The Savior's healing touch.

. . . As though he had read her thoughts, he lifted his hands and placed them firmly on either side of her head. He closed his eyes and began to move his lips in silent prayer.

A feeling of exquisite warmth rose inside Magdalene, filling her head as if the energy of life itself pulsed from Jesus' hands. She thought she felt his grip tighten on her head, and at the same time her body trembled, as though some unwanted force were leaving her and setting her free. She felt the trembling again, and again—five times, six times, seven—and then it stopped, and the most beautiful peace she had ever felt washed over her.

Slowly, Jesus removed his hands from her head. She opened her eyes to see him smiling at her . . .

The Woman Called MAGDALENE

A powerful and moving novel of faith and love!

Biblical Fiction
by Gloria Howe Bremkamp

Mara, The Woman at the Well

The Woman Called Magdalene

Phoebe: Paul's Messenger to the Church at Rome (Spring 1992)

The Woman Called MAGDALENE

Gloria Howe Bremkamp

CARMEL • NEW YORK 10512

Printed in the United States of America
This Guideposts edition is published by special arrangement with Gloria Howe Bremkamp.

Library of Congress Cataloging-in-Publication Data
Bremkamp, Gloria Howe.
The woman called Magdalene / Gloria Howe Bremkamp.
p. cm.
ISBN 0-89840-329-4
1. Mary Magdalene—Fiction. 2. Bible. N.T.—History of Biblical events—Fiction. I. Title.
PS3552.R369W6 1991
813'.54—dc20 91-13993
CIP

For Blanche and Charlotte,
who meant so much in my life

Author's Note

It has been said that those most favored of God often are those most maligned by men. So it has been with Mary Magdalene.

From the Middle Ages on to the present time in western cultures, the name Mary Magdalene has come to mean a "fallen woman." Now, more recent interpretations of Scripture, and more openness of scholarship, indicate that our western culture definition of her name may not be an accurate one. This is the premise on which this novel is based.

Soon afterwards he went on through cities
and villages proclaiming and bringing
the good news of the kingdom of God.
The twelve were with him,
as well as some women who had been cured
of evil spirits and infirmities:
Mary, called Magdalene, from whom
seven demons had gone out,
and Joanna, the wife of Herod's
steward Chuza, and Susanna, and many
others, who provided for them
out of their resources.

—Luke 8:1-3, New Revised Standard Version

She felt the heat of anger begin to rise in her face. Jesus turned and looked at her . . .

1

"MAGDALENE! HURRY! Before the Romans come back to steal more of our sheep." Her mother's voice pierced the cold, still-dark morning from the safe warmth of the house.

Magdalene made no effort to reply, but hurried faster toward the field to reclaim what was left of the flock. Hurrying along beside her were the two young shepherds who had been overpowered by the Romans, had watched them steal a dozen ewes and a prize ram, and finally had alerted the family about the disaster.

"Run faster, young shepherds. Run faster! The other sheep are straying," commanded her father who was following after her.

The boys sprinted forward carrying their shepherd's staffs like lances, whistling and calling out to the sheep, trying to calm them with the sounds of familiar voices.

If only they really had carried lances, Magdalene thought, the theft would not have happened. She wished for a lance for herself. She would put a stop to this thievery. Violence was something Romans understood. Fresh anger spurted inside her, fueling her dislike of their arrogance, igniting her resentment of their authority.

No one was safe from them. Not even Domenicus, who had curried their favor to avoid conscription into their army. But his efforts had been unsuccessful, and for the past three years he had been away in the service of the Romans.

She wished he were here now, in her place, in the black coldness of predawn, chasing frightened sheep. He belonged here. And she belonged in the safe warmth of the house instead of in a situation like this where her anger flared so easily and could go out of control so quickly.

Her "red-headed temper," as Domenicus referred to it, was not a thing to make fun of. It was such an awful anger, like some dark spirit-force of rage that turned her usually sunny disposition into one of stormy blackness. In those moments, it was as if some dark angel abruptly invaded and possessed her whole mind and body in some dark spell. When the spell was over, she was left trembling . . . and ashamed.

Abruptly she slowed her pace, trying to subdue the anger, knowing that she *must* subdue it, not wanting a spell to come upon her.

Her father caught up with her and stopped, his breathing hard and labored. He leaned over, bracing his hands against his knees to catch his breath that came in foggy bursts.

"If only Domenicus were here," she said, fearing for her father's over-exertion. "You and I have run far enough!"

It was a fool's chase anyway. The two young shepherds would round up the remaining flock. And those that had been taken would never be recovered. The Romans would hide them, or slaughter them so quickly that the theft could never be proven. Nothing could be done except to lodge another complaint with the centurion in charge of things at Magdala.

She pulled the hood of her cloak more closely around her head and face, thinking how little good it would do. The centurion was Rhodocus, a liar and a cheat and a thief himself. He would do nothing about the theft of their sheep, except to be more scornful of any disaster that befell her father's house. Justice from the Romans was a rare thing, even in the best of times.

Now it seemed to her that things were far worse than ever before. The Emperor, Caesar Tiberius, was in retirement on some island in the Great Sea. The empire was in the hands of Sejanus, one of his generals. A new governor had been sent out from Rome to rule over Judea, Samaria and Galilee. His name was Pontius Pilate. He was stern, militant, severe. The men under him all seemed to reflect the same characteristics. Things were worse than at any time she could remember.

Nor was she alone in this opinion. Most people who traveled the great trade route from Damascus to Jerusalem and stopped over in Magdala felt the same. Only recently a visiting trader had said to her father,

"Geshem, you're one of the fortunate ones. At least you're still a master of the guild of spinners and weavers in Magdala. In the towns and villages of the Decapolis, it's the Romans who lead the guilds and give the orders."

"It may seem that I am still in charge," her father had answered. "But in truth it was better before the Emperor Tiberius retired. This man Sejanus, and the men who follow him, are treacherous."

Treacherous indeed, Magdalene thought, still watching her father struggle to catch his breath. She hated what the Romans' authority was doing to his pride. She despised their callousness toward him.

Her father straightened, breathing easier now, and looked toward the field where the shepherds appeared to have the remaining sheep secured in a thornbush enclosure. "Dawn soon will come," he said. "And I will go to the Centurion Rhodocus and lodge a complaint about this thievery."

"It will do little good, my father."

He shrugged and turned back toward the house. "I must do it anyway."

"Then I will go with you," Magdalene said, walking along beside him.

"There is no need for that," Geshem protested.

"There is a need for me to go with you," she insisted.

"What need? Do you, too, think I no longer have the heart to deal with the Romans?"

She ignored his petulance. "Since my brother has been away, I share your work. I supervise your weavers.

I share in the profits of our family's business. I must also share the responsibility of dealing with the Romans."

He shook his head. "You will only lose your temper if you go."

A defensive silence settled between them. She knew he was right about her temper, and she feared the truth of that fact beyond all else in life. Especially when the anger boiled over and raged like demons out of control, and resulted in the strange spells that left her spent and weakened. Though she remembered little about them afterward, she knew that people were frightened by them and turned away from her because of them.

She had long since decided there were only two things she wanted from life. One was to be rid of the spells. The other was to find a man to love. She also had long since decided that life probably would give her neither.

Magdalene already was twenty-eight years old. None of the young men in town had sought a marriage contract, in spite of the fact that some of them found her attractive. At least, her brother Domenicus had said they did.

She was tall and slender, lithe and athletic. When she and Domenicus, just two years older, were children, she was the best athlete. But Domenicus would sneer and push her away. "You're only a girl. You can't play boys' games."

Long since, she had given up the games of childhood and had grown into a striking-looking woman with hair the color of spun gold, flecked with red. Her mouth was full and generous, quick to smile. Her eyes were a curious gray-green that seemed to change color with the blue of the sky or the grayness of a cloudy day. Her nose was aquiline, matching a straight jawline that spoke of courage.

But because of her affliction, none of the young men of the town ever sought to court her. And none ever sought out her father about a marriage contract. She was now nearing the end of her third decade, still living with her parents, still deeply involved in their lives.

The affliction also affected her friendships. Joanna and Susanna were the only friends who seemed unafraid when the anger unleashed itself so recklessly. They had been her friends since childhood, and never turned away from her because of the spells. But they no longer lived in Magdala. Joanna had married and moved to Jerusalem. Susanna had moved to Capernaum with her family. Magdalene now saw them only occasionally.

Aside from them, there had been only one other person who seemed unafraid of her anger and the dreaded spells. But she saw him even less frequently than she saw Joanna and Susanna. He was a young Jewish man from Nazareth, a carpenter who, with his father, built the sturdy wooden frames of the weaving looms for her own father's business.

Several times in past years, he had come to Magdala either to repair a loom, or to bring new looms to be assembled piece by piece right in her father's compound. The process always took several days, and the hospitality of her family's household always was extended to him. Since he was only a year or two older than she, they had become good friends. He was tall, strongly built with broad shoulders and well-muscled arms. He had a kind face but with rugged features, and his dark eyes always held a thoughtful look. He laughed easily. And he seemed genuinely interested in her.

"Why do they call you Magdalene?" he asked after first meeting her.

"Because Mary is my given name, as it is my mother's. But there are so many women named Mary that it is confusing."

"My mother, too, is named Mary."

"Yes, women named Mary are everywhere, it seems. To avoid confusion, my father started calling my mother by her second name, Hannah, many years ago. Few people even remember her by any other name."

"And they call you Magdalene because you were born here—in this city of Magdala?"

She nodded. "Strange name for a girl, isn't it?"

"I like it," he said. "It is different and special. As you are!"

His compliment was genuine. And he seemed equally pleased when he learned that she had been taught to read and write.

"That's different, too. Who taught you such skills?"

"My father. He is Greek, you see," she explained. "And knowledge means everything to a Greek."

"As religion means everything to a Jew," Jesus said with a soft laugh.

"I suppose. Anyway, when my father began to teach my brother Domenicus to read and write, I begged to be taught too. Domenicus didn't like it much. He would hide the parchment and quills so I couldn't practice writing."

"Then how did you learn?"

"By using a stick as a quill and writing in the dust of the courtyard."

"And how does your brother feel about it all now?"

"He still doesn't approve. He keeps saying that women don't need to know such things." She gave a sudden laugh. "But then, Domenicus has always considered himself superior. To practically everybody!"

Jesus joined her in her laughter, as if he, too, might have such a brother.

She basked in the warmth of his understanding and approval, and realized that the friendship she had struck with this carpenter from Nazareth was important to her simply because he didn't seem to think of her as inferior. He, too, was a very different kind of person. He was sensitive to others' feelings, yet he seemed unaffected, plain-spoken. He treated her with respect—as an equal. She tried to be with him as much as possible.

Sometimes they walked together along the shore of the great lake. At other times they sat and talked on the rooftop of her father's house. Often they sat with their parents and listened to them speak of great and worrisome things. During those times she often found Jesus looking at her with intense interest, as if trying to read her deepest thoughts. Instead of glancing away in embarrassment as she would have with the young men of the town, she felt no discomfort in meeting his gaze with a smile.

On one such occasion her mother noticed their

attentions to each other, and afterwards spoke sharply to her about it. "You do not stare back at young men, Magdalene. Young women of good manners simply do not do that."

"But my mother, we are friends. I like Jesus."

"Friends or not, you do not exchange such looks with a young man you barely know."

"I feel as if I've known him forever."

"Nonsense. Do as I say. Be a bit more restrained."

On another day during his last visit to Magdala, he went with her to fetch baskets of spun wool from the house of Janna. Two local boys coming from the fishing docks passed them and began to taunt Magdalene about her temper.

"Look! It's the mad woman of Magdala!"

She felt the heat of embarrassment, then anger, begin to rise in her face.

Jesus turned and looked at her.

The taunting continued. "Mad, mad, Mary!"

"Show us your temper, Mary!"

"Throw a fit, Mary!"

"Show the stranger what a fit you can throw!"

Two other boys joined them and began to fling themselves about in a grotesque mimicry of the contortions she made when the spells overtook her.

Anger flaming, she wanted to cry out in protest, as much against the panic of a seizure rising inside her as at the taunting boys. She began to tremble uncontrollably.

Panic.

Panic growing.

Seizure.

Blackness.

In a few exhausted moments, the blackness gave way to grayness and a feeling of warmth. She became gradually aware that someone was holding her firmly, comfortingly. The awful trembling stopped. She looked up. Her friend Jesus was holding her, watching her with concern and compassion.

Feeling strong enough to stand alone, she straightened, and saw her father running toward them. From the other direction came Janna, the wool spinner, who had a broom in her hand; and Dalphon, the fish merchant.

"A thousand apologies, Magdalene," Janna said, face flushed from the effort of chasing the boys away with her broom.

Dalphon joined the apology. "They did it deliberately. To embarrass you in front of your visitor."

"I am sure they succeeded," her father said grimly.

"You are better?" Jesus asked, slowly releasing his hold on her.

She rubbed at her forehead and nodded. "Thank you. I am all right now."

Later, at the close of the day, Jesus came to her on the rooftop of her father's house to speak about the incident. "Is it something you can talk about?" he asked in a gentle way.

"To you," she nodded.

He sat down beside her.

Even in the gathering dusk, she could see in his

face patience, genuine interest, and absolutely no fear. "I have been so afflicted for as long as I can remember," she confided. "My mother and father have consulted physicians. None of them seem able to help."

A shadow of pain seemed to darken his brow.

"I used to think if I could just control my temper, the spells would no longer happen. But . . . " Her voice trailed off into a miserable memory of trying and failing, trying again and failing again, periodically subject to temper, to anger, and eventually to the overwhelming spells.

He watched her as she regathered her thoughts. There was a hint of a sparkle in his eyes—that of a true friend who listens, who cares, and who loves the other without condition. He placed his powerful hand on top of hers and, without a word, gave her a reassuring smile as if to say, *I understand. I really do. And everything is going to be all right.*

Indeed, he was a true friend. Though he knew about her affliction and had witnessed it first-hand, he had not turned away from her.

The next day, Jesus and his father left Magdala to return to Nazareth. That had been more than two years ago. She had not seen him since. But she thought of him often, wondered how he was and what he was doing. She still puzzled over why she had felt such a sense of awe about him.

At every opportunity she had asked travelers from Nazareth if they knew of him. No one seemed to until recently, when a cloth merchant from Nazareth came to buy homespun.

"Jesus, the carpenter?" the merchant said in

answer to her question. "Yes, I know him. But he is no longer in Nazareth. He left some weeks ago. His mother and brothers are still there, but he has gone away."

"And his father?"

The cloth merchant shook his head. "Joseph? I believe he died many months ago."

Even now, as she walked back to the house, the memory of that news conversation sent a tremor of sadness through her. Jesus and his father had seemed to like each other very much. Joseph's death must have saddened Jesus. She wished she could have known and could have comforted him, as he had comforted her during his last visit. She glanced at her own father walking beside her in the cold gray light of half-dawn and realized how saddened she would be if anything happened to him.

Her whole life would be changed. That must have been how Jesus felt when Joseph died. Maybe that's why he left Nazareth. There had to be some important reason why he, an eldest son, would do such a thing. She wished she knew why. She wished she knew where he was. And she wondered if he still remembered her, or ever thought about her. It would be good to see him again.

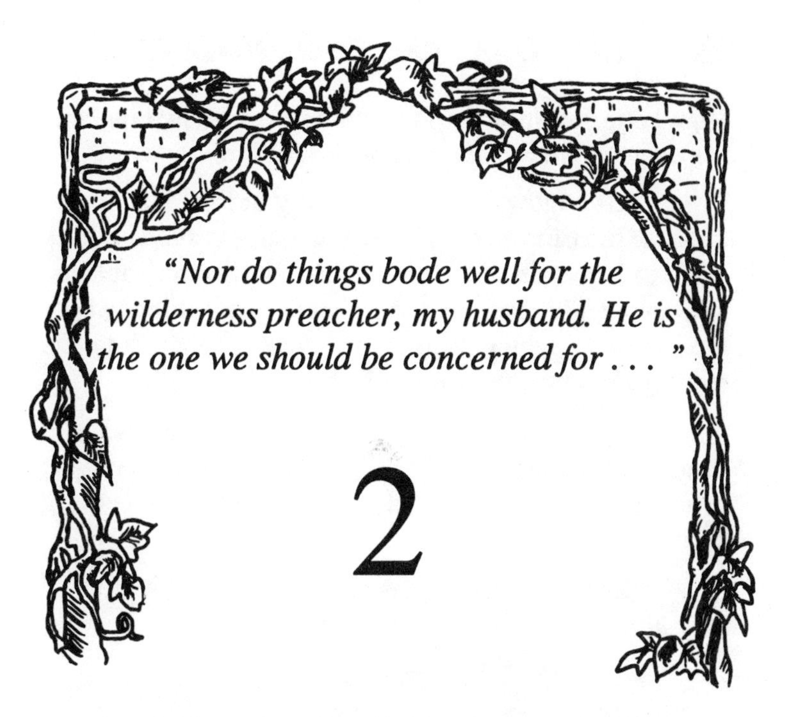

"Nor do things bode well for the wilderness preacher, my husband. He is the one we should be concerned for . . . "
2

THE PALACE OF HEROD ANTIPAS at Tiberias was a new one, as the city itself was new.

Only three years earlier, Herod Antipas had built the city on the western shore of the Sea of Galilee in honor of Rome's Emperor Tiberias. It was more than just an existing city renamed for an emperor. This was a completely new city built especially to honor Tiberius. Herod even hired Roman architects and builders. It occupied land that once was a sacred burial ground for Galilean Jews. But now, no good Jew would go near Tiberius. The city was an affront to them.

The site, of course, had been Herod's deliberate choice. He wanted to show the Romans how like them he really was, thinking that by so doing he would ease his tax burdens and enjoy more benefits from royal Rome.

How better to do it than to build a brand-new city over the bones of an old and conquered foe?

His strategy had worked only in part. His invitations for the Emperor to visit the new city availed nothing except a letter of thanks; no Roman of influential rank had yet visited Tiberias. And there were many things about the new city which were unsatisfactory, including the royal baths in the palace itself.

"By all the gods, why can't those Romans build these baths so they can be truly heated?" Herod Antipas fumed, stepping up gingerly from the shallow bathing pool.

Steam hovered in the pool's enclosure, but it was only a token. The water was tepid.

"Eumenes! Fetch Chuza!" the tetrarch shouted. "And bring him to me in my own chambers!" He pulled a toga from its peg on the wall, draped it around his swarthy figure, and headed for the doorway. Eumenes bent double in a bow of obedience and hurried off in the other direction.

Herod's servant Eumenes hated the early spring in Tiberias. It was always cold this time of year. Herod knew that. Why he insisted on coming here so early in the spring was a puzzle, for the bath was never hot enough for him. But there was nothing that Eumenes could do about it. He was a servant, not an engineer, and not one of the stokers who shoveled hot coals all around the water pipes to heat the baths. He hated it when the tetrarch raved and shouted at him.

Just ahead, Chuza, Herod's minister of finance

and household affairs, emerged from a doorway. Eumenes hurried faster to deliver the tetrarch's message.

"The baths again, heh?" Chuza said with a sigh of disgust. "They will never please him. The Romans built them on the wrong side of the palace. It's impossible to warm them enough."

"Yes, my lord minister, everybody in the palace knows that," Eumenes agreed. "But I cannot change it. Why does he yell at me as if I could?"

"Because you are at hand," Chuza said, not unsympathetically, leading the way to Herod's private chambers. "And he is yelling at you, and everyone else, because he is nervous about Pontius Pilate's visit."

By the time Chuza and the servant Eumenes arrived at Herod's private chambers, the tetrarch had wrapped himself in a heavy robe and was pacing about, flailing his arms for warmth. The toga lay on the floor where he had tossed it. "Why did we let ourselves be persuaded to come here so early in the spring? Why, Chuza? Why did we allow it?"

"This was the only time the new Roman governor would agree to come," Chuza reminded him. "And you wanted to impress him with your cooperation, your excellency."

"We'll impress him, no doubt. With chills and fever!"

"I understand that he is a man of great physical hardiness. He'll no doubt approve of the palace bath, sire."

"Have you tried that bath?"

"I bathe in the lake, sire."

A look of disgust crossed Herod's face. "Oh yes, I forgot. Well, I like a hot bath!"

Eumenes picked the toga up from the floor and went to a huge cupboard where the royal garments were stored.

"When is Pilate to arrive here?"

"Tomorrow, your excellency," Chuza said. "Rather early tomorrow, I expect. His aides tell me he is a very early riser."

Herod grimaced. "He would be."

"Everything is ready for his arrival," Chuza continued. "Foods, wines, the softest of linens for his sleeping chamber. And the Lady Herodias and Joanna have arranged suitable entertainment for the governor's wife, should he decide to bring her with him."

"What's her name?" Herod asked.

"Procula, sire. The Lady Procula."

He thought for a moment. "Herodias may have met her in Rome."

"That will be helpful."

"Pray that it is," Herod said, glancing at him with an uncertain look. "Who knows how she may feel about divorced women remarrying a brother-in-law? I'm glad your Joanna is here to help entertain the Lady Procula."

Eumenes returned with undergarments and tunic, and helped Herod to get dressed.

"You say that everything is in readiness?"

"Yes, your excellency. Even the royal barge has been readied."

Herod frowned. "It is too cold to sail."

"Pilate is fond of sailing, your excellency."

The tetrarch turned and narrowed his eyes.

Chuza shrugged. "If you want him as an ally, you must cater to him. Everyone tells me that."

By the time Pilate's entourage arrived the next day, Herod had decided to take Chuza's advice. He would cater to Pilate. Dressed in the most modest of all royal robes, he was diplomatic in his welcome to the governor; charming, but cautious, in his greetings to Pilate's wife, and agreeable to the two tribunes who served as the governor's aides.

He personally conducted the tour of the city, making certain Pilate saw all that glorified the Emperor Tiberius and Rome itself. He was generous with his comments about Roman architects and builders, and never once mentioned the tepid quality of the water in the royal bath.

On the final day of Pilate's visit, Herod even hosted a sail on the royal barge for a few hours. Pilate seemed to enjoy it. But when the talk turned to serious matters of government, of relationships with the Sanhedrin and the priesthood in Jerusalem, of requests for military assistance in the event of uprisings, Pontius Pilate was non-committal, even aloof.

"We Romans are peace-keepers," he said. "Nothing more. Even here in Palestine."

The Roman entourage departed from Tiberias later that same day, leaving Herod Antipas with unanswered questions about whether the building of the new city would have benefits for him.

"What do you think, Chuza?" he asked, walking slowly back into the palace. "Have we made an ally of Pontius Pilate?"

"Our wives might be able to give us that answer."

Herod stopped in sharp surprise.

Chuza grinned. "Astonishing, isn't it?"

"You think they really know?"

"I think it is most probable."

"Then let us go to them by all means, for Pontius Pilate has left me in great puzzlement."

They found Joanna, Chuza's wife, and Herodias in a far part of the palace that looked out over the Sea of Galilee. The first dark mists of evening bruised the sky beyond the mountains on the opposite shore. The water had taken on a glassy grayness. Water birds, singly and in pairs, silhouetted against the grayness before disappearing in the oncoming mists.

At the sight of the two men, Joanna stood up, bowed to Herod and gave a deferential nod to Chuza. She was tall, slender and fair-skinned, an obvious and interesting contrast to her husband, who was short and portly.

Herodias, on the other hand, was as dark as Joanna was fair. She acknowledged the appearance of Chuza and her husband, Herod, with a wave of her hand, and remained seated. "We were taking our rest," she said as Herod bent to greet her by kissing her hand. "After the past two days, we need some rest."

"You found the Lady Procula trying?" Herod asked, taking a seat beside his wife.

"Joanna liked her. But I found her a bore."

"In what way?"

Herodias shrugged. "In most every way."

Joanna and Chuza exchanged a knowing look. Herodias seldom liked other women. She was either envious or suspicious of them, depending on their rank. In Procula's case, Herodias's envy had been aroused.

"That's too bad," Herod said. "I was hoping you got to know her a bit. At least enough for her to tell you a confidence or two about—"

"A confidence?" Herodias straightened. "She didn't impress me as being the confiding type. She spoke only when spoken to, and then kept a careful and distant formality."

"Oh, I see." Disappointment edged Herod's voice.

Herodias asked for quick confirmation. "Didn't you find her to be formal and distant, Joanna?"

"Hm-m-m, yes, I suppose that could describe her."

Though she answered without hesitation, Chuza questioned her with a sharp look.

Herod stood up and paced away. "I wish there had been something to give you an impression of the governor through the eyes of his wife."

"Oh, I got an impression of him, all right."

Herod turned in anticipation.

"The impression I got is that he will never be your ally, my husband."

The look of anticipation turned to one of surprise.

"The impression I got is that Pontius Pilate

despises Palestine and everything in it, including the royal house of Herod."

A dark look covered Herod's surprise.

Herodias got up, went to the window and looked out. But she could not escape the darkness. By this time, it was almost full upon the face of the land, too. She turned again to face her husband. "The governor's lady despises me in particular."

"Why?"

"Because I divorced Philip to marry you."

The look of darkness deepened on Herod's face.

"She has heard about the wilderness preacher who proclaims that we live in sin, and that we have broken the customs of man and the laws of God."

Herod swore and turned away.

Chuza touched Joanna's arm and motioned that they should leave. She nodded and followed him toward their own chambers. Once inside their own rooms, he turned to her and asked her if what Herodias had said was true.

"It is true." Joanna took off her cloak and sat down on a small settee.

Chuza came and sat beside her. "Did the Lady Procula actually discuss that subject with Herodias?"

Joanna shook her head. "It came out in conversation almost accidentally. And certainly, it was overheard by accident."

"How do you mean?"

"Procula actually was talking with me. Herodias had gone to the baths. Procula was explaining how she was puzzled by the strange mix of politics and religion here in Palestine. She expressed sympathy for anyone who is the subject of rumors. She used the rumor about the wilderness preacher as an example. It not only was a most unfortunate choice, but she also said it at a most unfortunate time."

"Just as Herodias returned from the baths."

"That's right, my husband. And you know Herodias. Anything she can construe as criticism is criticism."

A look of consternation filled Chuza's round face.

"Procula is a very reserved lady. From the start of the visit, Herodias was cool to her. But after she overheard that one bit of conversation, she was absolutely frigid toward Procula."

"It does not bode well for the tetrarchy," Chuza said. "We may need Pontius Pilate's friendship one day. It does not bode well for that, at all."

Joanna reached for his hand, and held it in her own. "Nor do things bode well for the wilderness preacher, my husband. I think he is the one we should be concerned for."

He looked at her with a rueful smile. "It is not wise to hold such concern."

"Perhaps not," she said softly.

"There is no perhaps about it. It is not wise to hold such a concern," he repeated. "In spite of our own disapproval of Herodias."

"What about our own consciences? The wilderness preacher speaks of repentance and about the coming of a new kingdom. He uses Herodias and Herod as examples of what we must turn away from."

Chuza pulled his hand away from hers, stood up and walked toward the window. "I have lived with my own conscience as Herod's household minister for many years, Joanna. But things are different with Herodias in the palace. I must be doubly careful. And so must you."

His reaction was stronger than she expected. In the several years of their marriage, they sometimes disagreed about unimportant things. But not about things of the conscience. Chuza's sense of decency and fairness was what had first attracted her to him. He was a man of honor. He disapproved of the fact that both Herod and Herodias had divorced their first spouses to marry each other. He disapproved of it as much as she did.

Chuza turned toward her, his round face bearing a troubled look. "You had mentioned when we came to Tiberias that you would like to go on up to Magdala to see Magdalene and her family. Do you still want to go?"

She stared at him in open surprise.

"It's only a short journey from here to there."

The statement was true. And it was also true that she had told him she would like to visit Magdala while they were in Tiberias. But the timing of his question left little doubt that he felt she might become a political liability if she stayed on at the palace.

"Wouldn't you like to see Magdalene again? It has been quite some time since you visited her."

She looked at him without answering.

He came to her. "Please, my pet, Herodias will not let this subject rest. And when the confrontation comes over this wilderness preacher, I frankly do not want you involved."

In the next instant they were in each other's arms, laughing and crying, hugging and babbling all at the same time.

3

WHEN THE MESSENGER came from Tiberias with the news that Joanna would be coming to Magdala for a visit in three days, Magdalene was thrilled. Her friendship with Joanna went so far back that she could not remember when they first met. It had grown as they did, evolving and maturing in a way so natural and so comfortable that neither distance nor time had eroded its freshness and its joy.

Joanna had not been in Magdala since the death of her parents some time before. To Magdalene, just thinking about Joanna's coming once again was exciting. She set about at once preparing the household for the visit. Fresh reed mats were readied in the sleeping alcove. These were covered with the softest of new linens recently arrived from Egypt. The supply of foodstuffs was checked and rechecked. Servants were instructed to sweep the house and the courtyards with particular care.

Her parents, who thought of Joanna as a second daughter, joined in the preparations. The large brass torchier given to them some years earlier by Joanna and Chuza was brought out of storage, furnished with an extravagant brand saturated with tallow oil, and positioned in a prominent place in the main room of the house for extra light and warmth.

"While Joanna is here, we must make a special feast and invite all of our friends," Hannah said. "After all, she is married to a very important man."

"Have a caution, my wife," Geshem said. "Too much showing off may be unwise."

"Why? By all that is reasonable, why?"

"The Romans, for one thing."

"I said invite our friends. That doesn't include the Romans. At least, not in my mind."

"They will hear of it."

"Let them. We never invite Romans to this house."

"This situation is different," Geshem said.

"Different? How?"

"Different because of the political ties between Herod's court and the Romans."

"Nonsense!"

"It might even be politically good for our son Domenicus."

Hannah hesitated, pausing a moment to consider

her husband's last statement. Geshem turned to Magdalene.

"What do you think, daughter?" he asked.

"I think we should wait until Joanna arrives. She may not want a big fuss made over her."

"Nonsense!" her mother said. "Joanna always liked having someone make a fuss over her!"

Unwilling to argue, Magdalene turned away and walked from the house, across the courtyard and into the weaving rooms to select a welcoming gift for her friend. Six women weavers sat before their looms, working shuttle through warp. Magdalene selected a beautiful cloak of sheerest white wool from a stack of newly woven ones, and then stood watching the weavers, fascinated, as she had been since childhood, to see the fabric take substance and form. She and Joanna had both been taught to weave. She wondered if Joanna ever did any weaving now, or if her role as wife to an important royal minister kept her too busy for such a simple thing.

She would have to ask her. It would be another item to add to the list of things they would have to talk about, she decided, as she retraced her way across the courtyard toward the house. The main room was empty and quiet, but from a side area of the house where all of the cooking was done, she could hear her mother telling the servants that a special feast would be given in a few days, and instructing them about early preparations. Magdalene entered her sleeping alcove and put the gift cloak in a cupboard; then stepped outside the house to make sure the front courtyard had been properly swept.

A noise came from the gate. She turned just as the gate was pushed open from the street by a manservant wearing the royal crest of Herod Antipas on his tunic. He nodded to her and stood aside.

Joanna stepped into view. Tall, fair, simply dressed, she had arrived with no fanfare and only two servants, the manservant and a woman who stood close by, clutching a small traveling bag.

A rush of joyful excitement went through Magdalene. "Is it you? Is it really you?"

In the next instant they were in each other's arms, laughing and crying, hugging and babbling all at the same time. Magdalene thought her heart would break with the joy of it. She had not realized how much she had missed Joanna. Holding her at arm's length, she searched her face for any changes. Maturity had brought new strength to the angular jawline. But the look of openness and candor was still there, dominated by clear gray eyes.

They hugged again in delight while the two servants stood watching their reunion in silent approval. Passersby on the street turned to look. Two Roman officers peered at them with curiosity. One pointed to the crest on the manservant's tunic and murmured something to his companion before moving on down the street.

"Come in, come in," Magdalene said. "Welcome. Welcome." Arm in arm, she and Joanna crossed the courtyard and entered the house. The servants followed.

"Joanna!" Hannah exclaimed, hurrying in from the cooking area. "My child, how happy we are that you have come!" She embraced her, and called out loudly for Magdalene's father.

Geshem appeared from a side entrance, followed by Tobias, one of the household's servants. Joanna made a deep bow to him. He hesitated, surprised by such a show of high respect. Then with a hearty laugh, Geshem returned the bow. When he straightened, he motioned toward the servants and asked, "Who is this you've brought with you?"

"This is Razis. He is manservant to my husband. Chuza insisted he come with me. And this is Eglah. You remember her? She was with me when I was last here. In fact, she's been with me since Chuza and I were first married."

Both servants bowed.

Geshem acknowledged the introduction. "This is Tobias. He will show you where you are to stay. Are there others with you?"

Joanna shook her head.

"Where is your luggage?" asked Hannah.

She pointed to the small satchel which Eglah was carrying.

"Nothing more?" Hannah asked, astonished.

Joanna laughed. "Nothing more."

"But surely you plan to stay a while with us. How can you do so with no more luggage than that?"

Before Joanna could answer, Geshem went to the gate and looked out into the street. "Where is your carry-chair? And where are the bearers?"

"You're an important woman," Hannah said. "You should have more than two servants."

"And did you walk from Tiberias?" Geshem asked.

Joanna held up her hands in a gesture of helplessness at the barrage of questions. "I sailed from Tiberias to Magdala."

"Sailed?" Magdalene said in surprise. "You *have* changed, after all. I can remember when you wouldn't even step into a boat."

"The royal barge is a bit more steady than that tiny boat your brother Domenicus had!" Joanna said.

Magdalene laughed. Her brother's boat had been tiny. And not too safe, as she recalled, especially when Domenicus was in a reckless mood.

"How is Domenicus? And where is he now?" Joanna wanted to know.

"He's stationed at the Fortress Machaerus," Geshem said. "Do you ever visit there with your husband?"

"Chuza has been there. I have not."

"Refreshments! You must have refreshments," Hannah said, moving off toward the cooking area. "I shall see to them."

"And I must go check on the spinners and weavers. But we are glad to have you with us again," Geshem added. He left the room by a side entrance.

Joanna turned and walked around the room, examining it thoughtfully.

"The place has had few changes," Magdalene said.

"It is wonderful to be here again. Simply wonderful. What memories I have of this place! Memories that mean so much to me. Whenever things get bad, whenever I'm unhappy, I think of this place. And of you. It always helps."

"Are things bad now, my friend?"

"Why do you ask?"

"Something in your eyes . . . "

Joanna stopped her stroll around the room. "I am worried," she confessed, coming toward Magdalene. "I am worried about something that Chuza thinks I have no right to worry about." She took off her cloak, laid it aside, and sat down on a small settee.

Magdalene joined her.

"Have you heard of the wilderness preacher called John the Baptizer?" Joanna asked.

"Yes," Magdalene nodded. "What about him?"

"I'm afraid he is in danger. Or soon will be." She went on to tell Magdalene of the incident between Herodias and Procula, and of Chuza's prediction of trouble with the Romans for Herod. "The fact that I am concerned for the wilderness preacher disturbs Chuza. That's the reason for my visit here. He's afraid I will get involved. That's why he shipped me off to you."

"Then you didn't want to come?"

A startled expression crossed Joanna's face. Quickly she leaned forward and clasped Magdalene's hands. "Don't be silly. Of course I wanted to come. Before we left Jerusalem, I told Chuza I wanted to come here for a visit. But—"

"Yes?"

"But I wanted to come at my own time, and on my own terms. This way, I feel that—"

"You feel that Chuza thought you might be in the way?"

"That's it. That's it exactly. And it's a feeling I don't like. I don't want him to ever feel that way about me."

"I don't blame you for that," Magdalene said sympathetically. "But there is something about this I don't understand."

"What's that?"

"Why do you feel such concern for this wilderness preacher? I had understood he is Jewish, and a member of the Essene community. Do you know him? Is he a friend of yours?"

"No. I have never met John the Baptizer. His being Jewish doesn't matter to me, any more than it would matter to you. You know that."

Magdalene waited, wondering how Joanna could feel such concern for this wilderness preacher she had never met.

Joanna blushed, as if reading her thoughts. "I know it sounds silly. But I have been told what he preaches."

"And what is that?"

"That we should all repent. That a new kingdom is coming, and that we must repent to be a part of it."

"Well, no wonder Chuza is worried."

An odd look crossed Joanna's face.

"And no wonder he didn't want you involved."

"Magdalene!" Joanna said, a hint of hurt in her voice. "You of all people. I expected you to be on my side!"

"I am! I am on your side. And so is Chuza! He is

protecting you. He didn't just get you out of his way. He is protecting you."

Joanna sat back on the settee, folded her hands in her lap and, with a frown on her brow, studied them.

Magdalene knew the gesture well. Unless she chose her next words with care, Joanna would sulk. She sighed and shifted her weight on the settee. "You are right to worry about the wilderness preacher. You certainly are right about that." She glanced at Joanna to see the effect of her words.

But Joanna continued to study her hands.

"The Baptizer needs someone to worry about him. Open criticism of Herod's divorce and re-marriage is foolish, but preaching about some new kingdom that will compete with Herod and the Romans is openly dangerous."

Joanna looked up. A reassured smile broke onto her face. "So my husband's worry was not all centered on Herodias and Herod. There is more to it. How silly of me not to see that. And how silly of him not to say it like you did! I am so relieved."

"So am I," Magdalene said, meaning it. She had not expected a sad encounter so soon after her friend's arrival.

Hannah had returned to the room in time to hear the very last of the conversation. "Don't you two ever disagree about anything?"

"Never," Magdalene said, sneaking a sideways grin toward Joanna. Joanna returned the knowing look, and Magdalene motioned for the servants to place the baskets of fruit, bread and cheese nearby.

Hannah turned to Joanna. "The royal barge that brought you to us—"

"Yes? What about it?"

"I should love to see it."

Joanna laughed. "And so you shall. When it's time for me to return to Tiberias."

"You mean it isn't out there waiting for you?"

Joanna shook her head. "But it will return in a few days from now."

"A few days?"

"That's not a very long visit," Magdalene protested. "We shall hardly have finished talking!"

"Indeed, we have barely started talking," Joanna said. "And I have been doing most of it. Tell me about you, Magdalene. You look well. Are you?"

"Yes, I am well."

"Except for those spells," Hannah said.

"Please, my mother—"

"Nonsense! There's no need to hide anything from Joanna. She's like your own sister."

"It's of little interest . . . "

"The spells come less frequently," Hannah persisted. "But they seem to be harder. And they last longer. They also continue to frighten away an eligible husband. I'm afraid that Magdalene will never marry."

Magdalene stood and walked away, not wanting to turn Joanna's arrival into a recitation of her own ills, and not needing to be reminded that most men shied away from her.

Joanna, too, got up from the settee and went to

where the food baskets had been placed. “Magdalene, do you hear anything at all from Susanna?”

Grateful for the change of subject, Magdalene turned. “Yes, rather often. She still misses Magdala. But she’s made new friends in Capernaum. In fact, I think she has fallen in love with a fisherman named James.”

“Really? Our shy Susanna in love?”

“I think so. She sends messages from time to time that lead me to believe that is so.” Magdalene joined her friend at the food baskets and picked up some grapes.

“I’d love to see her,” Joanna said, selecting an olive.

“Why don’t we go to see her?” Magdalene asked on a sudden impulse. “Capernaum is not all that far away.”

“What?” her mother exclaimed. “But what about the feast I am planning in honor of Joanna?”

“Perhaps there will be time for both,” Magdalene said.

“Yes, of course there will be time for both,” Joanna said, winking in a way reminiscent of their childhood conspiracies. “If you agree that we can go to visit Susanna, then I will agree to be guest of honor at a feast for your friends.”

Hannah quickly agreed, and hurried off to find Geshem.

“That was very nice of you, Joanna. She wants to brag and show you off.”

“I know. I am flattered at such a welcome.”

“Oh, I almost forgot—” Magdalene turned suddenly, went into the sleeping alcove, and returned with the welcome gift for her friend.

"Magdalene, it is beautiful!" Joanna gasped, fingering the fine, soft weave, admiring the purity of its whiteness and the delicate blue design so deftly woven in the hemline. "Thank you. What a welcome, indeed."

"Do you think Susanna would like one too?"

"Of course! She would be as thrilled as I am!"

"Good. We'll take a cloak to her." Magdalene walked back to the settee. "In the meantime, I'll send Tobias with a message asking her if we can come to Capernaum to visit."

She had expected James to show a warm response to Susanna. But his reaction was not warm at all.
4

CAPERNAUM WAS A DAY'S WALK to the east of Magdala. By boat, the journey took only a few hours.

The city was an important one to the Romans. It was larger than Magdala, and stretched for more than a mile along the northern shoreline of the Sea of Galilee. North and east of the city, a major east-west trade route crossed the Jordan, linking the cities of the Decapolis with the Plain of Genesarett and with the north-south trade route that went through Magdala.

Capernaum's fishing industry was large and prosperous, and thus, important to the Romans. Susanna's father, Ephraim, who once had been a chief inspector of fish-buyers for the Romans in Magdala, had been reassigned to Capernaum when the chief inspector there had died. It was an important job and called for Ephraim to contract with all the major fishermen of the area for the large quantities of fish needed by the Romans for their garrisons at Capernaum, Beth-Julia and Gargassa.

One of the most prominent fishermen in Capernaum with whom he dealt was a Jewish man named Zebedee. With two of his sons, James and John, Zebedee ran a fleet of many boats and had in his employ many other fishermen. It was Zebedee's son James who had caught the attention and the heart of Susanna.

Magdalene and Joanna learned all of this on their first evening as Susanna's guests in her father's house. Their message asking if they could come for a visit had met with a delighted *Yes*. And so they set off on a chartered barge for the sail to Capernaum, accompanied by Joanna's servants, Razis and Eglah.

After the evening meal on the first night of their visit, Magdalene gave Susanna her gift cloak. And as Joanna had predicted, she was delighted with it.

"How beautiful!" she exclaimed. "It is so beautiful that when I wear it, James will think I'm beautiful!"

"When do we get to meet your friend James?" Magdalene asked.

"Do you really want to meet him?" Susanna blushed.

"If you want us to meet him, we'd like to," Joanna assured her.

"Oh, I want you to meet him," Susanna said, studying their reaction carefully. "But first I must tell you that he and his family are quite important here in Capernaum."

"I thought you just told us," Magdalene laughed.

"I only told you about the prominence of their fishing business."

"What else is important about them?" Joanna asked.

"They helped to build the synagogue here. There is an inscription on one of the columns that says so." Susanna's eyes were shining with pride. "Oh, I know that may not be important to you and Magdalene, but to my family, it is almost the most important thing about the house of Zebedee."

"Of course it is important to us, too, because you're our friend," Joanna said.

"It is a beautiful synagogue," Susanna explained. "Why, it has galleries for women on three sides. Can you imagine?"

"You must show it to us while we are here," Joanna said.

Magdalene nodded agreement, anxious to get back to what she considered more important. "But when do we get to meet James? When can we do that?"

"Tomorrow morning. Early. When the fishermen go down to the lake. Before they sail out for the day's catch. We will go then."

•

And so it was. They awakened, dressed in the dimness of one tallow oil lamp, slipped out of the house so as not to disturb Susanna's parents, and followed their friend to the place where Zebedee's fishing boats were drawn up on the sandy shoreline. When they arrived, they found several men already at work folding huge nets and stacking them into the boats.

"There he is!" Susanna exclaimed, pointing to a tall, bearded man near one of the boats.

He was with three other men, apparently involved in intense conversation.

Susanna waved at James.

He glanced up, hesitated, then with seeming reluctance waved back. The other men turned. The tallest one was a big, solid-looking man. The second was almost as large, but appeared to be somewhat older. The third man was the youngest of the three. He also was tall, but slender and clean-shaven.

"The one on the right is James's brother John," Susanna explained. "He is very nice too, but he's much younger."

"How old is James?" Joanna asked.

"Our age."

"Who is the big man?"

"His name is Simon. He runs the fleet that sails from Bethsaida. But his wife's family lives here in Capernaum. That's his brother Andrew standing next to him," Susanna said, watching James walk through the sand toward her. She pulled off her shawl, draped it around her shoulders, and self-consciously smoothed at her hair. "I wish I had worn my new cloak."

Magdalene moved closer to her. "You need no new cloak. I'm sure James already thinks you are beautiful."

James approached, looked at Joanna and Magdalene curiously, then turned a cautious smile in Susanna's direction.

Susanna, on the other hand, responded with such open adoration that Magdalene began to wonder if the relationship was not seriously one-sided. She had expected James to show a warm response to Susanna. But his reaction was not warm at all. And he, in fact, was not at all what she had expected. He seemed guarded, intense. Susanna was so shy and so naïve and so obviously in love that she probably considered James's intensity as strength.

"These must be your friends from Magdala," James said.

Susanna nodded, and in her excitement, became flustered searching for words.

Joanna stepped forward. "I am Joanna. This is Mary Magdalene."

He bowed.

Susanna recovered enough to say in an apologetic tone, "We have probably come at a bad time."

James nodded. "The day's work is just beginning. There isn't much time for visiting."

Susanna made a futile gesture with her hand.

"Maybe we can visit tonight," James said. "After the day's work, I'll come to your father's house. Tell him I need to speak with him."

Susanna nodded obediently.

James bowed again to Joanna and Magdalene, and walked back to where the other men waited. The four of them got into one of the boats and pushed out into the water.

"Isn't he wonderful?" Susanna said, pride in her voice. "I'm so glad he wants to come to the house tonight. Do you suppose he wants to speak to Father about a marriage contract?"

Marriage contract? Magdalene stared in surprise, wondering how Susanna could be so naïve. Or was it she who was wrong in her assessment of James? A glance at the surprise showing on Joanna's face reassured her that she was not wrong. Susanna was being naïve. To think that James was interested in marrying was as foolish as Magdalene thinking that her own physical condition would ever allow her to marry. It was a bleak and barren prospect. How odd that the two of them should share it. And for such different reasons.

"Maybe you should go and tell your father that James will be coming tonight," Joanna said.

Susanna hesitated.

"You did mention that your father often travels away from Capernaum," Joanna reminded her. "Shouldn't you make sure he will be home tonight?"

"I think he will be."

"But you want to be sure. If James is coming."

"Yes, of course. Let's hurry back to the house."

"You two go on," Magdalene said. "I want to walk by the lake for a while."

"I think I'll walk with Magdalene," Joanna said.

"Very well," Susanna agreed. "I will see you back at the house."

"Poor child," Joanna said, watching her go.

"Poor child, indeed. How has she convinced herself that he loves her?"

Joanna shrugged. "How do we tell her he doesn't?"

"I'm not sure we should tell her. Sooner or later she will discover it for herself. It's not as if there is no other man for Susanna. She will find someone else."

Joanna gave her a direct look. "And what about you, Magdalene? Is there to be no man in your life?"

"There has only been one who wasn't frightened of me." Magdalene looked out over the veiled distance of the water, remembering Jesus, seeing his face in her memory, recalling the sense of comfort he gave her, re-living the feeling of belonging when they were together.

"That boy from Nazareth? The carpenter?"

"You remember him?"

"I met him only once. But I remember him. I remember how he looked at you with tenderness and special friendship."

Magdalene smiled.

"Where is he? Do you ever hear from him?"

"Not lately." She began to walk along the shoreline. Joanna kept up beside her. The fishing boats were well out from the shore by now. Except for the soft crunching sound their sandals made against the sand as they walked, the morning was hushed and silent. The mountains beyond the lake's eastern shore still held back the warming brightness of the sun, and the air was still fresh with the mists of dawn.

Magdalene threw off her shawl and lifted her face

to the sky, welcoming the damp softness of the mists. "How I do love this great body of water," she said. "Even here in Capernaum. What peace I find just being near it."

Joanna agreed. "I had almost forgotten how beautiful it is. Especially here on its northern shore. Its moods are almost beyond understanding."

"They help to fill the emptiness of the soul."

"Yes," Joanna mused. "The lake gives solace in many ways, doesn't it?"

Magdalene looked at her friend with thankfulness. For more years than she could remember, she had found solace in sharing her deepest feelings with Joanna. She never feared that Joanna's approval of her as a person could be withdrawn, regardless of the raging anger that sometimes overtook her and produced the horrible spells. It was a comforting assurance, one she treasured.

"This lake, with all its moods, is like the soul of a woman alone. Especially when the winds from the northern mountains storm upon it and send it raging." Magdalene stopped. "That's when the sea is most like me, Joanna—when it is raging and out of control."

"Oh, my friend—" There was a note of plaintiveness in Joanna's tone. "Is it still so painful for you?"

"The lake and I are alike. I cannot deny it. But for all its storms, this is also where I find my peace."

Joanna drew close and put her arm around her friend. "Come back to Jerusalem with me. Let us find a physician who can cure you."

"Is there such a physician?"

"Somewhere. Surely, there must be such a physician somewhere."

By the time they returned to Susanna's house, the sun finally had scaled the mountain barrier to the east and had flung its net of brightness across the surface of the water. Susanna's mother, Rebah, had set out bowls of fruit and milk and small round loaves of brown bread. They ate heartily, appetites whetted by the fine morning air.

When they finished, they set off to the market with Susanna and one of the household servants to buy fresh vegetables for the evening meal. It was almost as it had been when they were girls together—shopping, bartering with the food vendors, examining fabrics and bangles, wrangling and haggling with shopkeepers about the price of their wares, chattering away about nothing of importance, and laughing at almost everything.

"It is so good to be together again," Susanna said when they arrived back at her house. "Sometimes I have wondered if such a thing would ever happen."

"Why should you think it wouldn't?" asked Joanna.

Susanna shrugged. "Well, with you married to such an important man and traveling everywhere with him. And Magdalene is so involved with her family's weaving business. And me—" she shrugged again. "What kind of a fisherman's wife do you think I will make?"

The question caught them both by surprise.

Joanna walked away, head down, lips pursed as if deeply considering her answer.

Magdalene answered the question with the first idea that popped into her head. "What are the duties of a fisherman's wife?"

"Well," Susanna said thoughtfully, "the first duty is to fix his meals and care for his clothes and clean his house and have his children and—"

"Those are the duties of any wife," Joanna said, looking at Susanna. "What are the special duties that James would expect of you?"

Susanna sat down on a nearby bench and stared gravely into empty air.

"You *have* discussed it with him, haven't you?" Magdalene asked, coming to sit beside her.

Susanna shook her head.

"Then what makes you think he will ask your father for a marriage contract when he comes to visit tonight?"

"You don't like him," Susanna said, abruptly turning toward her.

Magdalene straightened. "What do you mean I don't like him? What kind of a question is that?"

"Well, you don't, do you? I can tell."

"I have barely met the man."

"We have both barely met him," Joanna interjected. "How can we give you an answer to a question like that? You don't even know what he expects of you!"

"You're ganging up on me. Just like when we were girls." Susanna stood up and went out of the room into the courtyard, and appeared to find great interest in a huge, red hibiscus.

Magdalene followed her friend outside. "I'm sorry, Susanna. Please don't be angry."

Joanna also came outside. “We just don’t know James as well as you do.”

“You’ll be a wonderful wife whether the man is a fisherman or a shepherd or a—whatever,” Magdalene tried to reassure their friend. “You’ll be a wonderful wife.”

But Susanna kept her back to them, considering instead the great red blossoms on the hibiscus bush.

Joanna went to her and put her hand on her shoulder. “When I fell in love with Chuza, there was a time when I wondered if he really loved me. The wondering made me unhappy and it made me angry sometimes. Is that what your feelings are, Susanna? Are you wondering if James really loves you? And are you angry because you really don’t know the answer?”

Magdalene held her breath. Joanna had said exactly the right words. It was Susanna’s reaction she found bothersome. She remained with her back to them, shutting them out. Long shadows had begun to paint the courtyard. Beyond the walls of the compound, from down near the shoreline, voices of the returning fishermen could be heard calling to each other.

Finally, with deliberate slowness, Susanna turned toward them. She was holding two hibiscus blossoms. Eyes lowered and color flushing her face, she held out the blossoms and softly said, “I fear he doesn’t love me. That is my anger.”

Before either of them could react, Susanna’s father Ephraim opened the outer gate and entered the courtyard. “Ah, such lovely blossoms. Are they for me?” he teased. “Or are they for me to give to your mother?”

"They are a peace offering for Magdalene and Joanna," Susanna said.

Being a man of wisdom, her father simply nodded, smiled, and crossed the courtyard into the house.

Much later, deep into the hours of the evening, James finally came to the house. His greeting to Susanna was one of politeness and caution.

"He might as well be greeting his grandmother," Magdalene whispered to Joanna from their place at the far side of the room.

"Something else is bothering him. Listen." Joanna leaned forward to hear what James was saying to Ephraim.

"Some think the wilderness preacher may be the Messiah."

Ephraim frowned, moved to a bench near the firepit and sat down. With the houseservants long since dismissed, Susanna and her mother Rebah hurried to bring cups of wine to the men.

"Does this wilderness man preach that he is the Messiah?" Ephraim asked.

"No. That's what is so odd about it all."

"Odd? What do you mean?"

"He preaches that he is the messenger that comes before the Messiah."

Ephraim looked closely at James. "The messenger?"

James nodded.

"That comes before?"

James nodded again.

"Why does that trouble you?"

"Because it might mean the Messiah is already here."

Ephraim made a dismissive sound and turned to his wine.

"The wilderness man also preaches that a new kingdom is at hand," James added.

"That could be good for the fish business," Ephraim chuckled.

"You're not taking me seriously, are you?"

Ephraim's only response was a guarded look.

"You are like all the others I've been talking to," James continued, his tone intensifying. "You don't really believe there is to be a Messiah, do you?"

Ephraim studied the wine in his cup and remained silent. The reaction appeared to frustrate James even more. "You are not a good Jew, Ephraim of Capernaum," he charged.

A gasp escaped from Susanna. She started to rise, but Rebah restrained her.

"I should have guessed as much long before this. By your action in synagogue, I should have guessed. You are not a good Jew at all."

Ephraim's face reddened at the repeated insult. "You, James, are a foolish man." Ephraim's tone was deliberate. "You are arrogant and headstrong."

James bristled.

"You come to my house as a guest," Ephraim went on. "And yet you insult me. Your father, Zebedee, would not have such poor manners. Nor would he have such poor business judgment."

"Is that a threat?" James asked, getting to his feet.

Ephraim, too, stood. "It is a statement of fact. Beyond that, make of it what you will."

James turned, nodded curtly to the women and strode out of the house. The sound of the outer gate opening and closing rattled through the hush that had suddenly settled across the room.

Susanna began to cry.

Magdalene felt a weight of sadness settle in her heart for her friend. Poor Susanna. She doubted there would ever be a place for her in James's life.

On the other hand, what she had heard about the Jews' Messiah and a new kingdom ignited a spark of curiosity in her mind. She wondered if this was the same new kingdom that Joanna had said was now a worry for Chuza. If it was, she wanted to find out more about it. And she wanted to find out, too, where the Jews' Messiah fit into this new kingdom. Both Jew and Gentile would be affected by such a kingdom. And maybe even by the Messiah himself.

There, in the entry to the alcove, stood Rhodocus. He was looking at her with a strange hardness . . .

5

JUST HOW MUCH MAGDALENE, her family and friends would be affected by the Jews' Messiah, whoever he was and whenever he might come, was beyond all her imagination. But for the immediate time, she gave no more thought to the subject.

Instead, upon returning to Magdala, she and Joanna both were caught up in preparations for the feast which Hannah insisted on giving in Joanna's honor. The guest list was so large that the house, as spacious as it was, simply would not hold so many guests.

"There is no house nor hall in all of Magdala that can hold this many people," Geshem complained. "Must we invite so many?"

"You are the one who said we must!" Hannah

replied. "If we don't invite the Romans there will be plenty of room."

"We must invite the Romans," Geshem said. "I've explained it to you before. Joanna is a very important person because of her husband Chuza. As one of Herod's ministers, he works with the Romans all the time. We must invite the local Romans as a matter of courtesy."

"Courtesy, indeed," Hannah argued. "The local Romans show no courtesy to you. They have done nothing to help you recover our stolen sheep. They did not offer to pay damages or try to catch those responsible for the theft."

"We must at least invite Rhodocus and his aides."

Hannah scoffed.

"I might need his help in the future."

"Nonsense!"

There had been no end to the argument until Magdalene suggested they hold the feast in the courtyard of the compound. "It can be more like a reception, my mother. People can come and go as they wish. It need not be a formal dinner. You could even hold it in the late afternoon on the day following the Jewish Sabbath. And that way, you can invite all our Jewish friends who live in Magdala."

Joanna quickly agreed with Magdalene. Hannah accepted the suggestion and the final preparations went along much more smoothly. Everyone on the original guest list was invited.

The foods prepared were those that could be eaten with the fingers. There were no lentils or porridge dishes planned. An extra supply of wine was ordered for the occasion, and garlands of early blooming flowers festooned the courtyard with bright, joyous colors.

The day of the reception dawned equally bright and happy. The household servants were all dressed in new tunics purchased for them especially for the occasion. Magdalene and Hannah had new tunics, too. And Joanna wore her new white cloak that Magdalene had given her. By the ninth hour, guests began to arrive. City officials and the important people of the area were among the early arrivals. Most of them had lived in Magdala for many years and had known Joanna's family. There were tears of reunion and reminiscences. Other guests were merchants from surrounding areas who did business with Geshem. There was much laughter and telling of jokes.

Magdalene stood aside watching it all, pleased at Joanna's enjoyment, and relishing her mother's look of triumphant satisfaction as hostess of such an important event.

Near the tenth hour, the Romans arrived. Led by Centurion Aurelius Rhodocus, there were five of them altogether. When they appeared at the gate, the hubbub of talking and laughter abated. Many people turned to stare in surprise.

Geshem excused himself from a group of guests and welcomed the Romans. He bowed to Rhodocus.

The gesture was acknowledged with a curt nod.

Geshem turned to the others. "Come in. There will be many people here whom you already know. And there is food and wine. Help yourselves."

The four aides moved past him and headed for the

tables of food. "How is it that a sheepherder like you is acquainted with the wife of the honorable Chuza?" Rhodocus asked, examining the crowd in a calculating way. "Especially how is it that you know her well enough to have her as your houseguest?"

Geshem, man of good grace that he was, gave no sign that he found the Roman's rudeness irritating. "We have known Joanna since childhood. She is like a second daughter to us."

"A daughter, eh? That is interesting. And your—ah—your first daughter, is she here? Is she well enough to be here?"

"Well enough?" Geshem fended, feeling his irritation rise. "How do you mean that?"

Rhodocus gave a short laugh. "It is common knowledge that she has spells. Is she well enough to be here?"

Anger rose in Geshem's throat. He fought against it, wanting to retort but knowing he should not.

"And what a shame, too. Your daughter is really quite beautiful with that red hair and tall, slender body—"

"My daughter, Magdalene, is quite well," Geshem said carefully, more and more irritated at the tone of the Roman's references to Magdalene.

"I hope to see her today," Rhodocus persisted.

Geshem did not answer.

"I said I hope to see her today," Rhodocus repeated. "She avoids me most of the time. Why is that?"

Again, Magdalene's father did not respond.

Rhodocus turned abruptly and walked away toward the food tables.

Geshem watched him and swore under his breath at the idea that the Roman was interested in Magdalene. He watched Rhodocus accept a cup of wine from one of his aides, regretting that he had insisted on inviting him.

Tobias approached. "Master. The carpenter's son is at the back gate asking for the Lady Magdalene. Or for you."

"The carpenter's son? What carpenter's son?"

"The carpenter's son from Nazareth who used to come to repair the looms."

His memory refreshed, Geshem recalled the conscientious young man who had visited Magdala with his father. "Jesus? Invite him in, Tobias. By all means, invite him in."

The servant shook his head. "He doesn't want to intrude on the festivities. In fact, he turned away but I stopped him. I asked him to let me find you."

"Then I will go to him."

Magdalene saw them leave and was instantly curious. She excused herself from her guests and made her way through the crowd to follow Geshem and Tobias. She caught up with them just as they opened the back gate and stepped out into the street.

At first she didn't recognize the tall man standing just outside the gate. He was bearded. His shoulder-length hair was parted in the middle. His face was very tan, as if he had spent many days without shelter. He wore a long white tunic sashed at the waist with a narrow woven girdle, and caught up at the hemline with embroidered symbols used by Jewish rabbis. He was clean looking.

He smiled at her, his dark eyes alive with joy.

Joy surged through Magdalene as she realized it was Jesus. She gasped his name out loud.

His smile widened.

She rushed to give him a hug of welcome.

Her father, too, embraced him and said, "You must come in. There is food and drink."

"You must have some!" Magdalene said, hugging him again. "Oh, I am so glad to see you again!"

"Many of our friends are here," Geshem said. "They will remember you and be glad to see you, too."

"Even with my beard?" he laughed.

"Even with your beard!"

Magdalene took hold of his hand. "The festivity is in honor of my old friend Joanna, who is our houseguest. Please come in. At least for a bit of food."

A look of regret crossed his face. "I must be in Capernaum yet this day."

"But that's a day's walk," Geshem said. "Unless you're sailing, of course."

Jesus nodded. "I am. With friends who are fishermen."

"Can we at least give you food to carry with you?" Geshem asked. "As I remember, you always had a healthy appetite!"

Before Jesus could answer, Geshem and Tobias set off for the house to have a food bundle made.

"Can I not persuade you to come in?" Magdalene asked her old friend.

He shook his head. "Even though my time is short, I couldn't be near Magdala without stopping to see you. I have thought of you so often." His eyes met hers and held for a moment. "Are you well?"

"You mean the spells?"

He nodded.

"I am well enough. The spells seem to come less frequently now. But I still have them. I'm convinced it would take a real miracle to cure me."

A peculiar look flashed into his eyes, and was gone as quickly as it had appeared.

She wondered at it, reminded of the look of intensity she had seen in his face the last time they had been together and the feeling of awe it had brought to her.

"Much has happened to me since I last saw you," he said.

She pointed to the embroidered hemline of his tunic. "You are a rabbi now. That much I already know."

He nodded and smiled. "My life is different than it has ever been."

"I recently learned from a merchant that your father, Joseph, has died. I am sorry. I know how much you loved him."

For a long moment, Jesus was silent. His eyes searched her face in a kind, probing way, almost as if he were trying to decide how to speak of something that mattered to him even more than the death of Joseph.

She was puzzled by this, too. Nothing she could

think of should matter more deeply than the loss of a parent. Yet she felt sure that his reaction meant something of equal or greater importance had happened to him. What could it be? If there was just more time, they could talk about it. He could explain it to her. "Oh, how I wish you could stay with us for a while," she said. "I want to know about everything that's happened to you since your last visit here. What has it been? Two, three years?"

"A long while," he nodded. "Especially in terms of what has happened to me. I want to share that with you. And I will. I will make time to share it all with you."

"Promise?"

"Promise."

Geshem and Tobias came back across the courtyard and through the gate carrying two large bundles of food. "You will need no bowls or utensils for this food," Geshem laughed, handing one of the bundles to Jesus.

"That's very kind of you, sir. I thank you."

"Tobias will carry the other bundle for you to your boat. I would go myself, except for—" He motioned toward the far part of the courtyard.

"I have taken you away from your guests too long as it is. I will be coming back through Magdala soon. May I share your hospitality again then?"

"You are welcome in this house always."

Jesus turned to Magdalene. "Until later, may peace be with you."

She smiled at him in spite of a curious tightening in her throat. This is foolish, she told herself sharply. Why should she care so much? In reality, she barely knew him.

He bowed to Geshem and, with Tobias following, turned away toward the lake.

Magdalene went back through the gate, waited for her father to close it, and followed him across the court-yard in thoughtful silence. The torches on the courtyard walls were being lighted against the onset of nightfall. She wondered if Jesus and his friends would be safe sailing in the darkness.

The musicians began to play a lively tune. Several of the guests had formed a circle and were dancing. The chatter and hum of voices among the other guests grew. Here and there, laughter forced itself up even louder.

Magdalene suddenly felt tears against her face. How she wished her friend Jesus had stayed longer. How she longed to know all that had happened to him. Whatever it was, it had changed him. He had always been kind, but now she sensed an added strength in his kind-ness. He had always been different, but now there was a power, a presence, an authority about him that she had not noticed before. What was it that had changed him? It was something important. Something far more important even than her own realization that she might be in love with him.

In love? What could she be thinking of? In love indeed! She brushed at the fresh tears springing from her eyes, then searched the folds of her tunic for a linen square. Not finding one, she turned, leaving her father to rejoin the guests without her. She slipped quietly into the house by a side entrance and made her way to her sleeping alcove. She had just opened a small chest in which she kept accessories when a scuffling sound caused her to turn around.

There, in the entry to the alcove, stood Rhodocus. He was looking at her with a strange hardness.

She stiffened with fear—and with anger.

A loose, haphazard grin came to his face, but the hard look remained in his eyes. He made a drunken, mocking gesture of salute.

She moved to go past him out of the alcove.

He blocked her.

She moved to the other side.

He blocked her again. The grin on his face hardened. He grabbed both her arms and with unexpected strength, pushed her back into the alcove and down onto the stack of sleeping mats.

She fought, struggled against the weight of his body, wriggled to get free of him, despised the feel of the cold, hard metal fittings on the Roman cuirass that armored his torso from neck to waist.

He pressed down harder against her, insistent, demanding.

Panic caught at her already frenzied heart. She struggled harder. As she fought him, the stack of mats under her slipped sideways just enough so she could free one arm. With all the strength her fear and rage could summon, she brought the heel of her palm crashing upward into the base of his nose.

"A-a-gh!" He bellowed from the sudden shock and pain.

Magdalene twisted about, kicking and writhing to free herself entirely of him.

It was then that the other sensation welled up

within her. It was a familiar and unwanted feeling; one that signaled the onset of a dreaded seizure. She fell back as this much older enemy consumed her mind and body, leaving her completely vulnerable to Rhodocus.

Wave after wave of helplessness pummeled her, darkening the world, dragging her into an awful blackness. In the final instant before the blackness totally engulfed her, she saw Rhodocus's face. On it was a look of stark horror, as if he were witnessing the possession of a soul by seven demons from hell.

"You are now looking at a tribunal liaison," Domenicus announced with mock pomposity.
6

BY THE TIME THE SPELL had spent its fury and left Magdalene moaning in exhaustion, Rhodocus had disappeared. How long the blackness had imprisoned her was vague—an unperceived time that really didn't matter.

What did matter was that Rhodocus was no longer near her. A misty, hazy recall of the look of horror on his face swam up into her consciousness. She knew he had not harmed her, and she doubted that he would ever come near her again. What an irony that the horrible spell should have rescued her from his unwanted, and equally horrible, attentions. What irony, indeed! It was almost laughable, if only the reality of it were not so dreadful.

From the courtyard beyond the alcove and main room of the house, she could hear the music and the voices of the guests. The sounds came in waves of softness and loudness as she drifted in and out, back and forth on both sides of consciousness. She tried sitting up. But the pain in her head forced her to lie back down.

She rubbed at her forehead, pushing at the pain, willing it to stop until slowly it abated and she lay quite still, lulled by the fever-like sensation of drifting in and out of awareness.

When full consciousness finally returned, she realized that someone had placed a cool, damp compress on her forehead. She opened her eyes and found Joanna kneeling beside her, worry deep in her eyes.

"We must find a physician for you."

Before Magdalene could answer, her mother, followed by a houseservant carrying a fresh torch for the wall bracket, came hurrying into the alcove. Hannah sat down beside her daughter and took her hand. "Joanna's servant just came and told me. Your father will be along soon. He's bidding goodbye to our guests. It was a wonderful party, wasn't it?"

Magdalene nodded.

"My dear child, was there too much excitement? Did you get too weary? Was it the excitement of seeing our friend Jesus again? Your father told me he came."

Magdalene made a helpless gesture with her hands. "It is none of those things, my mother."

"This is the first spell she's had in quite some time," Hannah said to Joanna. "Is this where you found her?"

Joanna nodded.

"How is it that you were in here, Magdalene,

instead of with our guests?" Hannah rearranged the compress and smoothed it out across her daughter's forehead.

"On the way back from greeting Jesus, I came to get a linen square from the small chest there, and—"

"And—?"

"And that's when it happened," Magdalene finished, deciding against any further explanation. It would serve no purpose. Not now. She felt sure that Rhodocus would never admit to being anywhere near her. And it seemed more than certain that he would never bother her again. Why shouldn't she just keep the whole awful incident to herself?

But Joanna was looking at her in a compelling way, as if she suspected there was more to the story.

"I am all right now," Magdalene said softly, hoping to allay her friend's suspicions.

From the main room of the house, Magdalene could hear servants bringing in fresh torches for the house's wall brackets. She could also hear the sound of the outer gate being closed and latched. And in the next moment, her father appeared in the entry to the alcove.

"She is all right now, my husband," Hannah reported. "Joanna has seen to her for us."

"I would like to take her to Jerusalem," Joanna said. "They have many fine physicians there. There must be one of them who could help to cure her."

For a moment, Geshem stood looking down at his daughter, great sadness showing in his face. When tears abruptly glistened in his eyes, he turned and strode from the alcove.

Hannah rose quickly and followed after him.

Magdalene took the compress from her forehead, laid it aside and sat up.

"There is more to this incident than you have told, isn't there?" Joanna asked when she was sure her friend's parents were out of earshot.

Magdalene smoothed at her tunic, straightening it, and brushed her hair back from her forehead.

"Something else did happen, didn't it, Magdalene?"

"Yes—" As much as she wished to tell Joanna, the words halted in her throat.

"Were you assaulted in some way?"

She nodded.

"I thought as much! Who was it? That dreadful man Rhodocus?"

Magdalene stared at Joanna, her mouth open in surprise. "How did you know?"

"It wasn't hard, considering the way he kept leering at you in the courtyard."

"The way he leered at me?"

"I knew you weren't aware of it. But he kept looking at you in a most peculiar way. And shortly after you left the courtyard, he disappeared. I wondered where he had gone."

"Well, now you know."

"Did he harm you?"

Magdalene shook her head. "The spell came on too quickly for him to harm me."

"Chuza's Roman friends in Jerusalem shall hear of this!" Joanna's tone was resolute.

"No. You must not tell Chuza. You must do nothing."

"But Rhodocus must not—"

"He will do nothing more. He was terror-stricken—you should have seen his face! Please, you must do nothing."

With reluctance, Joanna agreed to keep the matter to herself.

The next afternoon, the royal barge returned to Magdala to take Joanna back to the royal palace at Tiberias. Hannah had changed her mind about wanting to see the royal barge, and bade Joanna farewell at the house, as did Geshem. So it was only Magdalene who walked to the docks with Joanna. The two servants, Razis and Eglah, walked behind them with Tobias.

Once more, the day was bright with sunlight and soft breezes. For Magdalene, the events of the previous day already seemed far past, except when her father insisted that Tobias escort her to the docks. It was then she realized how worried Geshem was that she might have another seizure. It was also then that she began to wonder if he somehow knew about Rhodocus, or whether Joanna had told him.

They reached the wooden dock where the royal barge was anchored. Razis and Eglah said goodbye to Tobias and bowed to Magdalene as they walked out onto the dock and boarded.

Joanna turned to embrace her friend. "I'm going to find a physician who can help you, Magdalene. When I do, I'll send a message. And you must come."

Magdalene hugged her in return. "I have loved being with you again. And thank you for caring for me."

"Promise me that you will come when I find the physician. Promise me."

"I promise."

"And promise me that you will tell your father about Rhodocus. You must. You simply must." Joanna turned away quickly and boarded the barge.

Slowly the craft pulled away from the dock out into deeper water. Then, with all oarsmen pulling together, it skimmed gracefully off into the haze of distance.

Magdalene watched it grow smaller and smaller. There was a sadness in her heart. She wished Joanna hadn't left quite so soon after the incident with Rhodocus. In fact, she wished Joanna hadn't left at all. She turned away and walked back to the house with Tobias.

To avoid her parents, she went straight to her sleeping alcove. She knew her mother would want to discuss every detail about Joanna's visit, about the reception of the day before, and about Magdalene's latest spell. But she didn't wish to talk. She had much to think about: Susanna and her adoration of a man who didn't seem to love her . . . the talk of the Jews' Messiah and a new kingdom . . . Joanna's concern for the wilderness preacher, John the Baptizer . . . the reappearance of Jesus and the changes in him . . . and Rhodocus . . .

In some way, she felt in her heart, each event would influence her future. She fell asleep wondering about them, and about what the future held for a husbandless woman her age who threw uncontrollable fits.

She was awakened some time later by the sound of voices. The sleeping alcove was dark. Only a small tallow oil lamp held back complete blackness. Beyond the alcove in the main room of the house, wall torches had been lighted. They cast flickering patterns of orange light. The voices were coming from there. She recognized two of the voices as those of her mother and father. But she struggled to identify the third. It was familiar, and yet—She sat up to listen more carefully.

One of the wall torches sputtered and flared into a greater pattern of orange, and at the same time the third person laughed. Instantly she knew who it was! It was her brother! It was Domenicus! The Romans finally had let him come home. She rose quickly and hurried to greet him.

He saw her as she entered the room, sprang to his feet and met her in a joyous hug. "Magdalene! You look wonderful." He turned to Hannah. "But you told me she had been ill."

"She has been."

"She doesn't look it."

"And you, too, look well, my brother," Magdalene interjected. Domenicus was heavier than she remembered him, but with his height, the weight was becoming. His red hair, cut short in the Roman fashion, had strands of gray in it, accenting a budding maturity that she also found becoming. She hoped it had subdued his recklessness. "How fine it is that you are home with us again!"

"It is only for a visit, I fear."

"I'm disappointed. We need you here."

"I know." He walked her back toward their parents and sat down beside her on a bench. Just beyond, a table was set with fruit, bread and cheese, a flagon of wine and wine cups for them all. "Father has been telling me he could use my help in running the family business. But I doubt that I can be helpful."

"At least Domenicus's new duties will allow him several days for visiting," Geshem said in obvious pleasure.

"New duties?"

"You are now looking at a tribunal liaison," Domenicus announced with mock pomposity, followed by a hearty laugh.

"A tribunal liaison? I'm not sure I know what that is. What does a tribunal liaison do?"

"Ah, my sister, you have not changed. You're still as full of questions as ever."

"It means he has been sent here to spy on Rhodocus," her father said.

"I work for a tribune who suspects that Rhodocus may be sending him false tax reports," Domenicus explained.

"I see."

"I was just telling our parents about it. The centurion in charge at Capernaum is also under suspicion. I am to check up on him too." He turned to Geshem. "Is Ephraim still in Capernaum?"

"He is. Magdalene saw him just a few days ago. She and Joanna were guests in the house of Ephraim," Geshem said.

"You mean Joanna has been here?"

Magdalene nodded. "She left only a few hours ago."

"I wish I could have seen her. Chuza never brings her to the Fortress Machaerus when he comes. And I never am invited to Herod's other palaces."

"Why do you ask about Susanna's father? Surely, Ephraim is not suspected of cheating your Roman friends."

"No, no. Quite the contrary," Domenicus explained. "I will need a friend in Capernaum to help me with my job. Ephraim would be just right."

"And who do you expect will help you here in Magdala?"

Domenicus looked at her sharply. Magdalene had put the question directly, but had not intended it to sound quite so critical.

"I expect he will ask me to help him," Geshem said, trying to soften the tension he sensed was taking hold.

Domenicus kept his eyes on his sister. "Is there some reason why I shouldn't ask our father to help me?"

"None at all." Magdalene rose from her seat beside Domenicus and went to the table. She picked a few grapes from a basket and nibbled at them, thinking of several good reasons why Geshem shouldn't help Domenicus spy on Rhodocus. For one thing, her father's leadership of the Spinners and Weavers Guild might be jeopardized. That would be a blow he could not stand. Helping Domenicus could make him even more subservient to Rhodocus's authority. But it was Geshem's place to tell that to Domenicus, not hers. She turned away from the table and discovered that Domenicus, Geshem and Hannah, all three, were watching her questioningly. She gave a small laugh, covering her real thoughts, and held out the grapes to them.

"Why is it you think our father shouldn't help me?" Domenicus pressed for an answer.

"I didn't say he shouldn't."

"You might as well have."

She brushed past him and sat down again on the wide bench, refusing to get caught up in an argument, especially so soon after her brother's arrival. His very words were in the pattern of their sibling arguments from childhood. Perhaps he hadn't matured as much as she first thought. But the idea that he would be in direct contact with Rhodocus did disturb her, especially in light of what had happened the day before.

"If you know of some reason our father shouldn't help me, you should tell me," Domenicus insisted.

"You're making something out of nothing, dear brother." Her tone was dismissive.

Color crept up into his face. "Perhaps the reason has nothing to do with our father at all," he challenged. "Perhaps the reason has to do with you."

She cringed inwardly, but met his accusing look without faltering.

"Nonsense!" Hannah reprimanded. "If there is a reason why your father should not help you, it has nothing to do with Magdalene."

Hannah's sharpness toward Domenicus caught them all by surprise. She never fussed at him. Whatever he did usually found favor with her. Except now. What had happened to cause this change, Magdalene wondered. Was it possible that her mother and father had somehow learned of Rhodocus's assault on her? Had Joanna told them?

"Your mother is right, my son," Geshem said. He rose and walked to the firepit, where he held out his hands for warmth. "Magdalene has nothing to do with this. I dislike Rhodocus. I have many reasons to dislike him. The most recent of which is his refusal to deal with those who stole our sheep."

Domenicus looked startled.

Geshem went on to tell him about the incident. "Because of this, I might not be of much help in your surveillance of Rhodocus. He would become suspicious at once if I were to help you."

Domenicus went to the table, poured a cup of wine for himself, gulped it down, and refilled the cup a second time.

For the next several days, he stayed in Magdala pursuing his surveillance of Rhodocus. He spoke no more to the family of his new assignment. If he asked Geshem to help him, no mention of that was made, either. His relationship with each of them was pleasant enough, but distant. It was clear from his actions that the family and its business were of no interest to him; and that the pursuit of his new assignment was his sole purpose for being back home.

Each morning he left the house early, sometimes before even the household servants had arisen to make the fires and begin the day's cooking. Most evenings he returned well after the family had retired. Some nights he didn't return at all.

"Domenicus is all Roman now, isn't he?" Magdalene heard her mother say to her father.

"Apparently so," her father replied.

"Have we lost him as our son?"

"I am not sure," Geshem said in a thoughtful tone. "But I think he already has made it clear that he finds the sheep business and spinning and weaving a dull livelihood. And I think he believes his best fortunes can be found with the Romans."

Her mother began to cry. "What will become of him? What will become of our firstborn?"

A sick feeling went through Domenicus.
Rhodocus and Magdalene?
Unbelievable!
7

ROMAN HEADQUARTERS IN MAGDALA occupied a large building near the Fish Tower, the magdal, which gave the town its name. Some of the Romans deridingly called the town by its Greek name, Tarichea. But most people called it Magdala and were impressed by such a handsome stone monument as the Fish Tower.

Domenicus himself was impressed by it. He had been so since boyhood when he longed to climb to its top and survey the world from that superior prominence. His father had never allowed him to do it. Neither had any of the Roman soldiers stationed at the towering pile of stones, who were responsible for lighting the beacon fires each night.

The beacons were a boon for travelers, both those coming in from the Sea of Galilee and those who traveled the road trailing down from the hills into the Plain of Gennesaret through the Valley of Robbers.

Domenicus stopped on his way to the Roman headquarters to look at the tower. It did not seem as tall as it had when he was a boy. Nevertheless, it was still impressive; and in a way, he supposed it symbolized the importance of Magdala itself. A city of considerable wealth, Magdala was a substantial agricultural, fishing, fish-curing, shipbuilding and trading center. And among the wealthy families of Magdala, his own ranked high. He was proud of that, in an off-hand way.

Geshem's ownership of large flocks of sheep, and his position of guildmaster of the weavers and spinners, gave his family the high ranking of prestige and leadership. Domenicus knew he could return to Magdala after his service with the Romans and find that same place of leadership waiting for him.

But he felt no desire for such a life. Service with the Romans had opened the eyes of his ambitions for power and wealth in a different way. It had stirred the fires of his passion for travel. Already he had been to Jerusalem, to the cities of the Decapolis, and to the coastal cities—even Tyre and Sidon. His next goal was Rome. His present visit to Magdala was nothing more than another step toward achieving his ambitions and satisfying his passion. But to return to Magdala permanently held no appeal.

He glanced up again to the top of the Fish Tower. The Roman sentry, who had been watching him with curiosity, waved a salute to him. He responded, then proceeded to the Roman headquarters and his first face-to-face meeting with Centurion Aurelius Rhodocus.

Domenicus had already formed an opinion of the centurion. From information given him by Tribune Fortunatus, he had concluded that Rhodocus was a prideful man and probably ruthless. Now his own observations of the centurion's reception hall confirmed that opinion. The hall was adorned with the trappings of violence and war; cudgels, spears, lances, swords, shields and daggers were on proud display. So was a set of battle armor, complete with cuirass, helmet and greaves. All were covered in a fine silting of dust, except for the cuirass. Apparently it had been worn recently.

Domenicus went to inspect it more closely. The strips of leather making up the corselet shone with use and had been waxed recently. The metal facings were polished. Domenicus wondered at it, since Rhodocus's job was an administrative one and not one requiring the wearing of battle armor.

The sound of approaching footsteps caused him to turn. Several legionnaires passed by the open doorway and on into the loggia. Two of them glanced at him, but they did not pause.

Then there appeared in the doorway the man he had come to see, the man he had been ordered to investigate. Centurion Aurelius Rhodocus was tall and lean looking. A thin, half-arrogant smile creased his face. A feeling of instant dislike coursed through Domenicus. This was a man to be doubly cautious of.

He saluted formally.

"Who are you?" Rhodocus asked without returning the salute.

"I am Domenicus, the tribunal liaison. I am also of the house of Geshem here in Magdala."

"If you have come about your father's sheep—"

Domenicus quieted the centurion with an impatient hand. "My father's sheep do not concern me. I am here on other business."

The Roman eyed him quizzically and proceeded on into the room.

Domenicus waited while Rhodocus circled him, taking his measure, calculating what risk was involved. "You move like a stalking lion, centurion."

Rhodocus looked at him sideways. "Why are you here?"

"On a matter of great seriousness."

Rhodocus paled.

Domenicus reached into the folds of his tunic and withdrew a scroll on which his orders had been written. "The Tribune Fortunatas at the Fortress Machaerus has reason to believe that you have a thief and a traitor working for you," he said, handing the scroll to Rhodocus.

Rhodocus seemed visibly relieved, and the color returned to his face. They were small signs of nervousness, but noticing them made Domenicus wonder what the Roman had expected to be accused of. It had to be something more than an investigation to rout out a thief. Unless, of course, the thief was Rhodocus himself. He thought again of what Fortunatas had told him about Rhodocus: "He's clever, deceitful and ruthless. Be on your guard."

Domenicus walked to the far side of the room where the arsenal of weapons was displayed, and inspected them. None had been used recently, though the dagger in its scabbard should have been if the cuirass had been worn as he suspected. But all were covered with the fine silting of dust he had noticed on the greaves and the helmet. Was Rhodocus really a man of violence, he wondered, or a passive coward who surrounded himself with the weapons of violence?

Across the room Rhodocus found a chair, sat down, and carefully read the scroll again. "I doubt there is a thief under my command."

"Fortunatas is not likely to be wrong."

"Where did Fortunatas get his information?"

Domenicus shook his head.

Rhodocus sat in silence for a long moment, a glum look masking his face.

Domenicus waited and watched, more and more certain that something other than Fortunatas's accusation was bothering the centurion.

At last, Rhodocus turned. "Why didn't Fortunatas send this message by courier? Or by Imperial Post?"

Domenicus shrugged.

"Why did he choose you as his messenger?"

"He wants me to help you find out who the thief is," Domenicus replied quickly.

"You're not a regular legionnaire, are you? You're a conscriptee?"

Domenicus nodded.

"Is Fortunatas aware of that?"

"I think he is. Why?"

Rhodocus pushed himself up out of the chair and paced across the room, wagging the scroll in the air.

"Conscriptees are not generally trusted with such a delicate matter as this."

Domenicus felt a knot of tension tightening in his stomach as Rhodocus pressed on.

"I doubt you really came from Fortunatas."

"You know his seal?" Domenicus countered.

"I do. But I also know that seals can be duplicated."

"You are refusing my help, then, to discover your thief?"

Rhodocus wagged the scroll in the air once again. "Until I can send my own courier to the Fortress Machaerus to confirm this, I shall need neither your help nor your presence in this headquarters. You are dismissed." The centurion turned on his heel and disappeared through the doorway.

It was a move Domenicus had not expected. He stood trembling with anger at the insult, disbelieving how quickly Rhodocus had turned the situation to his own advantage. Never before had his authority as tribunal liaison been so shattered or his sense of self-worth so trampled.

His official authority could be repaired by sending his own message to Fortunatas. Restoration of his self-respect was another matter. He had been humiliated, and he could feel the flames of embarrassed anger burning in his face as he strode from the reception hall to leave the headquarters.

As he paused outside to put his helmet on, some legionnaires were climbing the steps to the building. As they passed, he heard one of them say, "That's the brother of Rhodocus's woman standing out there."

"Rhodocus's woman?"

"Yes. You know. The one he brags about having all the time. The redhead. Magdalene. You know, the woman they call Mad Mary."

"Magdalene is Rhodocus's woman?"

"Why do you look so startled?" the first man said. "She's beautiful. And Rhodocus, after all, is the centurion in charge!"

A sick feeling went through Domenicus, overflowed his anger, filled him with revulsion. He took off his helmet and rubbed at his head. Rhodocus and Magdalene? Unbelievable! Then, suddenly, he remembered the conversation about whether Geshem should help him investigate Rhodocus and his mother's reaction in defense of Magdalene. Was it true that his sister and Rhodocus were lovers? And did the whole family know about it? Why hadn't they told him? Why hadn't they warned him? Why didn't they tell him that his own sister was whoring after a Roman?

He descended the steps two at a time and ran toward his father's house. He found his mother in the courtyard sewing. "Is it true?" he demanded, stopping in front of her.

She glanced up at him in surprise.

"And if it is, why didn't you tell me?"

"Do not shout so, my son."

"Why didn't you warn me?" he insisted. "You knew I would be confronting Rhodocus. Why didn't you tell me?"

Magdalene appeared in the doorway, attracted by the shouting. "What is it Mother should tell you?"

He spun on his heel and glared at her. "You! How could you?"

"How could I what?"

"Is it true?" he demanded.

"Is what true?"

"About you and Rhodocus!"

She sagged against the doorway for an instant, then straightened, lifted her head and walked resolutely toward him. "Is what true about me and Rhodocus?"

"Do you sleep with him?"

"Domenicus!" Hannah was on her feet, outraged.

He advanced on Magdalene, asking again. "Do you sleep with Rhodocus?"

Magdalene laughed. "Did he tell you that?"

Domenicus hesitated. He had expected denial, maybe tears, but not a laugh of derision as if such a thing could never happen.

"My son, you should know better than that!" Hannah said.

"How should I know better?" Domenicus charged. "How should I know better when I hear soldiers talking about my own sister as if she were a common prostitute of the streets?"

Magdalene couldn't believe what she had just heard. Her mother's face went white.

"You should know better. Magdalene is your sister," a voice said from the doorway.

They all turned.

It was Geshem. With a dark look of censure on his face, he came to Domenicus. "My heart grieves. You should have instantly put aside such an outrageous charge."

"But her reputation, Father! The reputation of this house! My reputation! Ruined!"

"There is no ruin to a reputation for those who know your sister, or for those who know this house. As for your own reputation—"

"But Father—!"

"You have been away from this house too long," Geshem said. "You no longer have any interest in our business. That was obvious from the first night you returned. Now it seems that you have no trust in your family. My heart grieves."

A sense of defeat seemed to temper Domenicus's anger.

"Besides, what can you do to stop Rhodocus if he wishes to tell such lies?"

Slowly, as the others watched him without speaking, logic resurfaced in the young soldier's mind. He remembered how swiftly Rhodocus had turned him out, choosing to ignore the authority certified by Fortunatas. Why then should a woman's reputation matter to such a man? And a woman who had seizures, at that.

"Very well, Father, I accept your reasoning. But I think you should do something about Rhodocus."

"That is not my job," Geshem said. "That is your job."

Defeated, Domenicus turned away. At the door,

he hesitated and said over his shoulder, "I shall be leaving for Capernaum when the sun rises next."

That her friend Jesus could be the spearhead of a treasonous movement was beyond comprehension . . .

8

THE AFTERMATH OF THE SCENE with Domenicus left Magdalene trembling in angry frustration at the thought of being called "Rhodocus's woman." It was as bad as being called a "woman of the streets," she told herself, watching Domenicus leave the courtyard and go into the house. She wished that somehow he had had enough trust in her to disavow such a charge. But then he had never been a trusting person. Why should she expect him to vouch for her now?

She turned toward her parents. The anguish in their faces was deep and full. It came to her that they still knew nothing of Rhodocus's assault on her, which made their anguish tear at her own heart even more. Joanna had kept her confidence. Perhaps that had been a mistake. Perhaps she should have told them at once about the attack. At the time, she was fearful of what her father might attempt in retaliation; beyond that, she had felt that nothing realistic could be done about it. It would have been her word against that of Rhodocus.

A sharp breeze suddenly cut through the courtyard. She shivered against it. It would still be her word against that of Rhodocus, she decided. Only now if she told what had really happened, Domenicus would most likely do something reckless to salvage his own pride.

Her father came to her. "Your mother and I regret this deeply, Magdalene. We will do what we can to stop this awful lie."

"Thank you, my father. But I doubt that you can do anything to stop it."

"The important thing is," her mother said, coming and embracing her, "that we know it isn't true."

With sunrise the next morning, Domenicus left Magdala for Capernaum to pursue his assignment as tribunal liaison. For the first time since he had come home, Magdalene felt a real sense of relief. Even though he planned to be gone for only a few days, she welcomed his departure.

The days rolled past in an even succession of supervising the weavers, taking long walks along the shore of the lake (accompanied by a watchful Tobias), sewing with her mother, wondering about Susanna and James, missing Joanna, and thinking about her friend Jesus. No further mention was made of Rhodocus or the lie he had spread about her. Domenicus was mentioned only when a courier from the Tribune Fortunatas arrived with an important-looking sealed document addressed to him.

When Domenicus himself finally did return from Capernaum, he brought a letter from Ephraim addressed to Geshem. In careful phrases that would not offend his old friend, Ephraim described Domenicus as an "aggressive and tenacious man who has outgrown us all. He appears to be obsessed with the successful pursuit of his assignment for the Romans."

Her father read aloud from the parchment for Hannah's benefit, then laid it aside, though there was much more to the letter, and left the room. Hannah followed.

Magdalene picked up the letter, curious about the rest of its contents, and began to read where her father had stopped.

> Domenicus reminds me of another man who has recently moved to Capernaum. This other man, too, has an obsession. He, too, like Domenicus, is aggressive and tenacious in the pleading of his cause.
>
> But this man's cause is not that of the Romans. This man's cause has to do with a new kingdom and the coming of Messiah. You will remember that I, your old Jewish friend, often spoke with you about our Messiah. Because this man's obsession has to do with that, he will become an enemy to Domenicus. In fact, he may already be his enemy. I find that regrettable since Domenicus seems to need friends, not enemies, and because he tells me he knows the man, as do you.
>
> The man's name is Jesus-bar-Joseph, the carpenter from Nazareth.

Stunned at the mention of Jesus' name in Ephraim's letter, Magdalene let the parchment slide from her hands onto her lap. That her friend Jesus could be the spearhead of a treasonous movement was beyond comprehension. To think of him as aggressive and tenacious was unbelievable. To liken him to Domenicus was unthinkable. Surely, Ephraim must be mistaken, his information wrong, his judgment faulty.

She rose from the chair and went in search of her brother. He was alone in a small storage room adjacent to the weaving rooms, looking through a stack of newly woven cloaks.

She waved the parchment to attract his attention.

"Ah, Magdalene. You have read Ephraim's letter, I see."

She nodded. "Did you see Jesus in Capernaum?"

"I did. On several occasions."

"And you spoke with him?"

"Of course. About many things."

"Did he mention having been here to see us?"

"Yes, I think he did mention it."

Disappointment curled through her at Domenicus's casual answer. She had wished for something more. "Are Ephraim's words about Jesus true?"

"So far as I can tell." He pulled a cloak from the middle of the stack, held it up and inspected it. "Is this a handsome cloak for your brother?"

She nodded, not giving a fig about a cloak for him. "Do you think Jesus is your enemy?"

He slipped the cloak over his head, adjusted it over his shoulders, and smoothed at it. "Would it make a difference to you?"

"Yes, it would make a big difference."

"Why?"

"Because I like him. And because you are my brother."

Domenicus stopped smoothing and straightening the cloak. "Which is more important?"

"What?"

"Which is more important? Your liking Jesus or my being your brother?"

"Couldn't they be equally important?"

He shook his head. "It will have to be one or the other."

"Why?"

"Because Jesus is a heretic."

"Domenicus!"

He glanced at her in surprise. "Believe me. Jesus is a rebel. He's a fanatic. And the men he has persuaded to join him are fanatics, too."

"What men?"

"Well, Susanna's friend James, for one."

Her heart sank, remembering the spark of intensity she herself had noticed in James's eyes. Could Ephraim be right about Jesus, or was he reacting to him by association because of James's abrasiveness?

Domenicus was looking down, checking the length of the cloak.

"The length is good," Magdalene said absently.

Her brother pulled off the cloak and tossed it

aside. "How is it that Susanna thinks James is in love with her?"

Magdalene shook her head. "Who are the other men following Jesus?"

"James's brother, a young redheaded lad. They call him John. And there's the big man from Bethsaida. His name is Simon, I think. Or maybe it's Peter. I heard Jesus call him Peter. And there's his brother Andrew. Then there's a guileless-looking fellow named Nathanael, another named Jude, a man from Emmaus called James the Lesser. And let's see—" He paused, thinking.

Magdalene went to the stack of cloaks, handed Domenicus the one he had tried on, straightened the rest and sat down on them.

"There are two or three others. One is named Judas from Keroit. Another is named Thomas. I rather liked him. He questioned everything that Jesus said and did." Domenicus paused, folded the cloak over his arm. "Then there was a man named Philip. One named Bartholomew. And one of our own tax-collectors, a man named Levi. I did some thorough checking on him. He changed his name to Matthew. I thought I had better find out all I could. About him and the rest of them."

"And what did you find out?"

"I found out that Jesus calls his men 'the twelve.' They call themselves his 'disciples.' One, or all of them, seem to be with him constantly. They travel everywhere on foot, or sometimes by boat. And wherever they go, great crowds follow to hear Jesus preach. And to watch him heal people."

Magdalene turned in surprise. "Heal? Jesus heals people?"

"Isn't that a laugh?"

She probed her brother with a puzzled look. "Why should such a miracle be laughable?"

He looked at her oddly. "Miracle? Come, come, Magdalene. How could a carpenter's son heal anyone?"

How indeed, she asked herself. She rose, paced to the doorway and stared into the adjacent room at the looms Jesus and his father had made. They were beautifully crafted—sturdy, practical, serving a good purpose in this world. But they were more than that, she felt. They were somehow like symbols of the kind of man she had perceived Jesus to be. Had she been wrong?

Or had real changes occurred in Jesus? And if they had, were they so radical in nature that he now served the purposes of a different world? Had Jesus always been aggressive and tenacious, and she just had not noticed?

Domenicus had called him a heretic and a fanatic. Peculiar, she thought, that she should remember nothing like that about him. And yet she remembered again and with clarity her impression of James as a fanatic. And he was following Jesus. Did that make Jesus a fanatic too? And what of this report that Jesus could heal people? Could he really? How could he do it? How did he do it? And if the report was true, did the ability to heal make him a fanatic?

In the next instant she realized that whether Jesus was a fanatic was beside the point. What mattered was his ability to heal. And what mattered even more was whether he had the ability to heal her!

"You're very quiet," Domenicus said.

She gave a startled gasp, then laughed at herself and turned back to him.

"Your thoughts must have been very far away."

"Yes. They were."

"You surely don't believe those rumors that he is a healer!"

"Oh, but Domenicus," she cried, her heart exploding with the very hope of the idea. "What if he is? What if my friend Jesus is a healer?"

"Magdalene!" Domenicus scoffed. "Not even you could believe such a thing!"

"But think what it would mean!" she whispered. "Think what it would be like to never again have those awful spells."

A peculiar expression crossed his face. "Jesus can't heal you! I should never have talked of him with you." He got up and left the storage room.

She watched him go, disliking the swaggering walk he had adopted from the Romans, and knowing that whatever he thought about Jesus or his healing powers really shouldn't matter. It was what she believed that should matter. After all, Jesus was her friend. Not his. She hurried back into the main part of the house and into an alcove which contained her father's writing table.

A basket of parchment scrolls and writing supplies was nearby. She pulled a small leather stool up to the writing table, mixed charcoal and water in a shallow bowl, selected a scroll and a quill and wrote:

> Joanna, dear friend.
> I have found the man who can heal me.
> He is presently in Capernaum.

I want you to be with me when I go to see him.
Can you come quickly to do that?
Magdalene

She rolled the scroll into a tight cylinder shape, sealed it with her father's seal, tied a small leather thong around it, and went to find Tobias.

"This is for the Lady Joanna," she said, handing him the scroll. "She can be found at Herod's palace either in Tiberias or in Jerusalem. It must be carried to her by our most trusted courier."

Tobias bowed. "I will send Jabuk."

"When can he leave?"

"This very day."

"Good. Tell Jabuk to wait for the Lady Joanna's reply."

Her body trembled, as though some unwanted force were leaving her and setting her free . . .
9

JOANNA'S RESPONSE to Magdalene's message was quick and certain. Yes, she would come to Magdala. And she would arrive within three or four days. Magdalene did not yet tell her parents about her plans. There would be plenty of time for that after Joanna arrived. She would tell them all at the same time.

In the meantime, she began gathering as much news as she could about Jesus. Staying busy with such activities was the best way she could think of to contain her impatience until Joanna arrived. It was also the only way she could contain the excitement and joy she felt even at the mere prospect of being healed.

She asked the weavers who worked for her if they had heard about a healer in Capernaum. Three of them had, but only one of the three believed the story to be true.

Taking one of the household servants with her, a young woman named Ramah, she visited Janna the wool spinner who heard lots of gossip, and learned that people were talking about a rabbi called the Nazarene. That had to be Jesus, she thought.

"He speaks much like John the Baptizer," Janna said.

"How do you mean?" Magdalene asked.

"He preaches a message of repentance. And he preaches that a new kingdom is at hand."

Magdalene thanked her and proceeded toward Magdala's only synagogue. There she made her way up into the women's gallery and listened intently for some word about Jesus from his own people. She heard little that satisfied her, and decided that the marketplace might be a better listening post. Appearing to shop, she and Ramah went slowly from booth to booth, listening carefully to the conversations of other shoppers and people on the street. Her efforts were soon rewarded.

A heavy woman in a bright blue shawl asked a companion if she had heard the wonderful news about the healings that were taking place at Capernaum. "My mother's cousin saw a paralytic healed," the woman said.

"Do you believe that?" her companion asked.

"Why not? My mother's cousin does not lie."

Two men dressed in the rough clothing of fishermen were talking together nearby. The older-looking of the two said: "Things are changing. The fishing business is changing. I fish for Zebedee of Capernaum now. Two of his sons have left him to travel with a rabbi from Nazareth."

The younger man looked puzzled. "Is he the same one that heals people?"

"That's the one. They call him the Nazarene."

Turning back toward her father's house, Magdalene overheard part of a conversation between a merchant and a legionnaire.

"There may be truth to the rumors about this man called Jesus," the legionnaire said. "He may be a healer. He might even be the Jews' Messiah. But I hear that he is a rebel and a heretic, and a friend of John the Baptizer."

"Then he best beware, or Herod will toss him into prison, too."

The more Magdalene heard, the more deeply she dredged for memories of every word Jesus had ever said to her. The deeper, too, went her thoughts about her destiny. She had never thought of herself as a religious person. Nor were her parents particularly religious.

Of all the gods she knew about, the God of the Hebrews was the one she felt most comfortable with simply because of her friendship with Susanna and her family. He somehow seemed the most personal of all the gods.

She remembered Susanna often praying to him about her problems or when she wanted something. Magdalene herself had prayed to him once about her spells. But she still had the spells. And she supposed his unresponsiveness was the result of the fact that she didn't understand all the Jewish rituals required for worshipping him.

On the other hand, the Romans had too many gods. They had one for every occasion, it seemed. It was too confusing, and somehow shallow. She wondered abruptly how Joanna felt about the Romans' gods; and how she felt about the Hebrew God, for that matter. How strange that they had not discussed it during her earlier visit. They had been close to the subject when they talked about John the Baptizer. But when Joanna came this time they would talk about it. Surely Jesus, now being a rabbi, must be close to the Hebrew God. Yes, they would need to talk about it.

Magdalene also began to wonder what Joanna would think when she learned that Jesus was the healer they would be going to see. She would only remember Jesus as a very young man helping with the looms. Would she believe that he could now be a healer? Or would her reaction be like that of Domenicus—cynical and scoffing? And what about her parents? How would they react? Should she tell them or not?

She dreaded the hue and cry that Domenicus would raise. And deep in her heart, she hated to raise false hopes in her parents' minds. It might be the better part of wisdom, she decided, not to discuss her plans with anyone except Joanna. That meant she would have to intercept Joanna before she arrived at the house.

As early light scattered the night shadows and brought on the day of Joanna's arrival, Magdalene slipped out of her father's house and made her way to a sheltered spot at the back of the weaving rooms where she could watch for her friend. Ramah, the servant girl, was with her. They settled down between a sycamore and an oleander bush to wait.

In front of them, the land gave way into a gentle

slope toward the shoreline of the lake. To their left, the town spread eastward, its piers and warehouses accented by the upward thrust of the Fish Tower. Beside it bulked the Roman headquarters, the hippodrome, the market places and the residential areas. To the right, a few scattered fishermen's houses were situated in a broken string along a narrow stream awash with snowmelt from the northern mountains. Beyond was where the trade routes intersected on the Plain of Gennesaret.

The wait for Joanna was shorter than she expected. Sunlight had barely started to animate the lakewaters with shimmering riffles when she saw the royal barge skimming toward Magdala's piers.

Ramah saw it at the same time and pointed. "Shall I go and fetch her for you, my mistress?"

"I think we both will go," Magdalene said, standing up. It was then she saw Domenicus leaving the house and heading toward the town. She grasped Ramah's arm before she could step out of the shrubbery into plain view. "On second thought, I think we will wait here for the Lady Joanna."

The servant gave her a puzzled look, but stood obediently still and quiet.

"Whatever you may hear me say to the Lady Joanna, Ramah, you are to repeat nothing. Not to anyone. My parents and brother know nothing of my plans. It will only upset them to know. Do you understand?"

The girl nodded, and then said in her soft, gentle way, "It has something to do with your friend Jesus, hasn't it?"

Magdalene looked at her and smiled, then sat back down to wait for the royal barge to dock and discharge its passengers. Within another few minutes she saw Joanna, followed by Razis and Eglah, coming up the slope. She stood up, stepped out into the roadway and greeted her friend with open arms, and led her back toward the oleander shelter. Razis and Eglah followed.

Joanna, surprised, glanced about them. "Why all the secrecy?"

"Because I don't want Domenicus or my parents to know the real reason you have come back, or why we are really going to Capernaum."

Joanna's eyes widened with surprise.

"It will only complicate things," Magdalene said.

"Then why have I come back? What have you told them?"

"I've told Domenicus nothing. I've told my parents that Susanna has summoned you—has summoned both of us—that she needs our help."

A grin broke onto Joanna's face. "She's having trouble with James, eh?"

"Something like that."

"Very well. But who is the physician you have found?"

"It is a long story. I'll tell you on the way to Capernaum."

They went on into the house then. Joanna's greetings to Geshem and Hannah were warm and without incident. But curiosity was pushing at Joanna about who the healer was. She pulled Magdalene aside and suggested that they go on to Capernaum as soon as possible. After the refreshment of a meal, they departed.

Once on the water, they settled themselves comfortably on cushioned seats in the bow of the barge, away from both servants and crew members.

"Now tell me," Joanna said. "Who is this healer you have found?"

Magdalene looked at her carefully, wanting to see every reaction that registered on her friend's face.

"Well—tell me your long story. Who is your healer? What is his name?"

"His name is Jesus. Jesus of Nazareth."

Joanna stared at her in astonishment.

The slip-slap of the water against the bow accented the moment, emphasized the silence brought on by astonishment, underscored the disbelief and the questioning Magdalene saw creeping into her friend's eyes. Her confidence faltered. It was the kind of reaction she had expected from Domenicus and her parents. It was the kind of reaction she wanted to avoid.

She reached out, clasped Joanna's hand, and began to explain before the questions could be voiced. "Yes, it is the same Jesus you met at our house years ago. And yes, it is the same Jesus, the carpenter, who came with his father to work on our looms. But he is not the same Jesus you remember. He is now a rabbi. He is now teaching and preaching and healing all around Capernaum. Hundreds of people are following him. Many have been healed by him."

"And there is no doubt in your mind that he can and will heal you."

"There is no doubt."

Joanna's questioning look vanished. She

squeezed Magdalene's hand. "Then from what I understand, it will be done."

It was Magdalene's turn to feel surprise. "From what you understand?"

Joanna nodded.

"That means you have heard about him too? That means you, too, know of Jesus' healing powers?"

Joanna nodded again. "I began to hear about him right after I received your message that you had found a man to heal you. Jesus is the talk of Herod's court. Only recently, one of Herod's noblemen who lives in Cana came to Chuza and reported that his son had been healed by a man named Jesus. I wondered then if it might not be Jesus of Nazareth."

"The nobleman and his son weren't Jewish, were they?"

A puzzled look crossed Joanna's face.

"What I mean is—" Magdalene stumbled, embarrassed that such a thought should have come to her. "Well, after all, Jesus is a Jewish rabbi, and I thought that—"

Joanna smiled and shook her head. "No, Herod's nobleman from Cana is not Jewish. And from what I understand, such a thing as a person's background makes no difference to Jesus. Jew, Greek, Roman. He reportedly has healed all kinds."

"Then you don't think I'm foolish to seek him out?"

"Just the opposite," Joanna replied. "I would think you foolish if you did not seek him out. He is your friend. And if he has this extraordinary power, you should ask him to help you."

Reassured, Magdalene settled back against the cushions to ride for a time in silent anticipation of her meeting with Jesus; yet she did not even dare to consider what it might be like to be healed, to never again have to fear the dreaded spells.

Joanna plumped up one of the cushions for herself and laid down against it. There was no wind, except for that stirred by the movement of the barge. From below deck came the muffled cadence-call of the boatswain to the oarsmen. Rhythmically tied to it was the plish-plash of the oars that broke the surface of the water to propel the barge along its intended route.

They were not far out from the shoreline. It was clearly visible with its strand of white sand and random clumpings of trees and shrubs. Beyond the sand rose a slope of hills, green and gentle. For a brief time the two friends dozed, lulled by the rhythm of the oars, comforted by the smoothness of the barge's movement, embraced in the euphoria of their journey and its purpose.

A shout from the bargemaster roused them. They sat up, looking shoreward in the direction he pointed. One of the hills appeared blanketed as if in hoarfrost, its greenness transformed by the presence of hundreds of people cloaked in white garments.

"What is it?" Joanna asked the bargemaster. "Who are those people?"

"They are people who follow the new prophet."

Magdalene looked at Joanna. "Does he mean Jesus?"

Joanna nodded.

Magdalene's heart sank. "How will we ever get to him? How can we find him in all that crowd?"

"Don't be afraid. We will find him. Susanna and her family will know where to find him," Joanna said. She stood up and turned to the bargemaster. "Can we go faster? Can we get to Capernaum ahead of the crowd?"

He bowed to Joanna, bent down and signaled the boatswain. The rhythm of the oars increased. The barge moved faster, passing the crowd, leaving them behind in a blur of white.

A few minutes later, Magdalene saw the first outbuildings of Capernaum. Then, as more and more of the city came into view, she recognized a part of the shoreline where she and Joanna had walked when they visited Susanna earlier. A number of fishing boats appeared, some far out on the water, their nets still adrift. Others were making for the piers and the shoreline. The barge slowed, its helmsman taking care not to swamp or collide with any of the smaller boats, and gradually made its way to a dock.

As soon as they could, Magdalene, Joanna and their servants disembarked and made their way to the house of Susanna's parents. They were greeted by a startled Rebah, who ushered them into the house, made them welcome, and explained that Susanna had gone up into the hills to hear Jesus preach.

"She will return soon. I am glad you two have come."

"Is Jesus staying here with you? Or with the fishermen?" Magdalene asked.

"At present, he is staying at the house of the

mother-in-law of Simon. Or Peter, as Jesus has been calling him."

"And where is her house?"

"Not far. Off to the east of here near the shoreline."

"Will Jesus go back there tonight?"

"I suppose so," Rebah shrugged.

"Will you direct us to that house?"

Rebah looked surprised. "You wish to go now?"

"Yes," Magdalene answered. "We wish to go right away."

With another shrug, Rebah got up, led them out into the street and pointed in the direction they should go. "You can't miss it. Simon, or Peter I should say, has built a shade on one side of the house out of old fish nets. No other house in Capernaum has such a thing. The rest of us use palm thatch."

They found the house without difficulty. The area shaded with fish nets faced the lake. A bake oven was built nearby. Smoke poured from it, almost hiding the old woman who crouched in front of it. They waited until she finished and stood up, then Magdalene greeted her, introduced herself and Joanna and asked where they could find Jesus.

The creases of age in the woman's face smoothed as her face broke into a smile. "So, you are Mary Magdalene. Jesus has spoken of you."

The news pleased her.

"I have not seen him since he left this morning.

He was going up into the hills to preach. My son-in-law and the others went with him."

"We saw the crowds," Joanna said.

"Ah—" the old woman hesitated and thought for a moment. "Well, then—I suspect you can find Jesus alone near the spot where the Jordan comes into the lake." She turned and pointed. "There is a place filled with willows and soft grasses. He often retreats there to get away from the crowds after he has preached. Just follow the shoreline. You will find him."

"Maybe we shouldn't disturb him," Magdalene said.

The old woman gave a soft laugh. "He will not be disturbed at the sight of you, Magdalene! He will want to see you."

Magdalene looked at Joanna. "Shall we go?"

"Come back for a meal in my house," the old woman called after them.

By the time they reached the area where the River Jordan flowed into the lake, the day was beginning to wane. Shadows cast by the westward-drifting sun were long. Their own shadows stretched out in front of them in comic elongation and teased them to remembrance of a childhood game of stepping on shadows. They began to laugh at playing the game even as they walked toward the willow grove where they hoped to find Jesus.

He heard their laughter and stood up.

Joanna saw him first and grabbed at Magdalene's arm. "Is that man Jesus? The one standing just this side of the trees?"

Joy flooded through Magdalene. "Yes, that's Jesus." She waved and ran toward him, filled with the beauty of him and already comforted by a sense of protection at the very sight of him. But halfway there, she remembered that though he was still her friend, he was a different Jesus now. And she was different, too. She had come on a serious cause. She should approach a rabbi who could heal her with dignity. She should not throw herself at him like some enamored girl. Magdalene slowed her pace.

Joanna caught up with her. "Is something wrong? Are you not feeling well?"

"I am all right," Magdalene said.

"Why did you slow down so abruptly?"

"I just realized what a serious thing I am asking for."

"Are you afraid?"

"Of Jesus? Never." She went forward once more, her eyes focused on his face. The closer she drew to him, the more aware she became of a new sense of strength and authority about him. She had first noticed it when he stopped in Magdala on his way to Capernaum. But here, in this peaceful place, she was aware of an overwhelming presence of power.

Jesus opened his arms to embrace her. Instead, she took his hands and knelt before him.

At once, Jesus lifted her to her feet. "Do you no longer seek me out as a friend?"

She gave a startled gasp.

"I suppose I shouldn't blame you. After all, I did

promise to return to Magdala to tell you all that has happened to me."

"But you have your work here. Important work."

"Then you have heard."

"I have heard. I have heard about your preaching and teaching and—"

"And she has heard of your healing, too. That's why we have come," Joanna said.

"You are Joanna? Magdalene's friend?"

Joanna nodded.

"I remember you," he said. "I have always thought how good it would be to have a friend I could feel close to as Magdalene feels close to you."

Joanna blushed at the praise. "I remember you, too, as a boy. And now I am impressed with what I hear about you as a man. So is Magdalene."

"Who told you about the healings?" Jesus asked, turning again to Magdalene.

"Domenicus."

"And still you came to me?"

"You have always been my friend. Always, I have trusted you. I still do."

Jesus paused a moment, gazing into Magdalene's eyes with a warm look of compassion. She remembered seeing a similar expression on his face more than two years before, when they had talked in Magdala following one of her seizures. She had felt reassurance then, a special peace of knowing a friend cared for her and accepted her in spite of her adversity. Now she felt the same sense of reassurance. But then, something was different too. Jesus was different. He was grasping her hands with greater resolve, and this time his gaze seemed to penetrate through her anguish and excitement to her very soul.

And it was in this moment that Magdalene knew, deep within her heart, that what people had been saying was true. Her friend Jesus was more than another carpenter, more than another rabbi. He was what people had been saying, and more. And he could indeed heal her.

As though he had read her thoughts, he smiled and released his grasp on her hands. Then he lifted his hands and placed them firmly on either side of her head. He closed his eyes and began to move his lips in silent prayer.

A feeling of exquisite warmth rose inside Magdalene, filling her head as if the energy of life itself pulsed from Jesus' hands. She thought she felt his grip tighten on her head, and at the same time her body trembled, as though some unwanted force were leaving her and setting her free. She felt the trembling again, and again—five times, six times, seven—and then it stopped, and the most beautiful peace she had ever felt washed over her. She closed her eyes and drifted with the beauty and the ease of it. A happy lightness held her suspended, supported her with an unexplainable strength and sense of well-being.

Slowly, Jesus removed his hands from her head. She opened her eyes to see him smiling at her. Joanna was staring in astonishment.

In an incredulous tone, Joanna whispered, "Demons left you, Magdalene! Demons! Seven of them. I saw you tremble as each one left. They are afraid of Jesus. They will not come back to you. Ever! They know you belong to him."

Tears filled Magdalene's eyes. Jesus smiled at her and brushed at the tears with his fingers. "Your faith has brought the healing power of my Father to your body. Your faith, my friend, has made you whole."

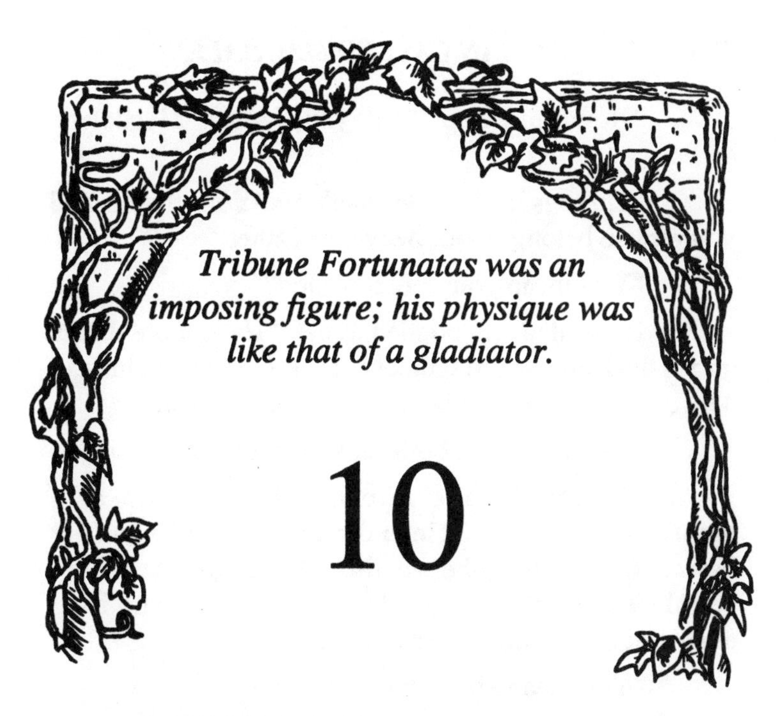

Tribune Fortunatas was an imposing figure; his physique was like that of a gladiator.
10

SOBBING IN RELIEF and ecstasy, Magdalene fell prostrate on the ground at Jesus' feet.

Jesus knelt in a prayer of thanksgiving.

Joanna went to Magdalene, her heart brimming with the joy of her friend's healing and awed at the power of the act. She knelt and placed a steadying hand on her friend's shoulder.

The soft gray of evening filtered across the land. The lake grew placid, mirrored moon silver.

When Magdalene's sobbing ceased, Jesus got to his feet and helped the women up. "Our friends in Capernaum will be wondering about all three of us, I suspect. If I remember Susanna's father, he will send a search party for us unless we return soon." He turned and, walking between them, led the way back toward the city.

"How can I ever thank you, Jesus?" Magdalene asked.

"There is no need to thank me. Your thanks and your praise belong to our heavenly Father."

"You mean your Hebrew God?"

He smiled and nodded at her. "He is more than a god to the Hebrews, Magdalene. He is God. To all human beings. He is love, and he is the power that heals."

She and Joanna both looked at him in surprise.

"I should have returned to Magdala as I promised," Jesus said. "I intended to tell you all about my Father, and about all the wondrous things that have happened since I last saw you at your home. It would have made understanding easier for you."

"You mean about my healing?"

He nodded.

"But I accept that I am healed," she said softly.

He put his arm around her shoulder and gave her a hug. "Your faith is deep, Magdalene. You are one of God's own."

"As you are?" she ventured. "Was that what you wanted to tell me?"

He nodded again. "I and my Father are one. The prophecies as written in the Torah are now being fulfilled."

They walked on together in a silence broken only by the occasional cry of a night bird or the song of a fisherman far out on the lake. Magdalene smiled to herself, aware of a sense of lightness—an inward, physical sureness she had never before experienced. The newness of the sensation mingled with her sense of awe at the idea of being healed. She looked at the lake, feeling as placid as the surface of the water appeared to be, and knew deep in her soul that she need never again compare herself with the lake when it was stormy and angry with waves.

The news of Magdalene's healing passed quickly among the believers in Capernaum. Susanna and her family hosted a celebration of joy, with all of Jesus' men, the house of Zebedee and Peter's wife and mother-in-law as invited guests. Ephraim sent one of his servants to Magdala with the wonderful news and an invitation for Geshem and Hannah to come and join the celebration.

"So that's why she and Joanna went to Capernaum!" Hannah exclaimed. "Why didn't she tell us? Why couldn't she have let us know what her plans were?"

"You don't really believe that she is healed, do you?" Domenicus demanded. "Healed by a carpenter's son?"

"That's enough, Domenicus," Geshem said, placing a comforting hand on his wife's shoulder.

Domenicus persisted. "My mother, how can you be so gullible?"

"That's enough, I said," Geshem ordered. "Whether or not you care to believe it, such miracles are possible."

"But my father, surely—"

"Your mother and I choose to believe that it has happened. We are accepting Ephraim's invitation and are going to Capernaum. You are welcome to come with us to see for yourself whether the healing is real."

Domenicus shook his head. "I am expecting the arrival of the Tribune Fortunatas, remember? According to the message he sent, he should be arriving any day now. No, I cannot go with you. I will be needed here."

On the second day after Geshem and Hannah departed for Capernaum, the Tribune Fortunatas and two aides, Marcus and Justinius, arrived in Magdala. Fortunatas was an imposing figure of a man. Though only of medium height, his physique was that of a gladiator. And he had the demeanor of a man accustomed to having his own way. He came by this naturally. His family in Rome was an important one. His father was a senator; his uncle a legate to several provinces in Syria.

When Domenicus had informed him of the rude reception Rhodocus had provided, and of his refusal to allow access to the garrison and its records, Fortunatas had responded that he would come personally to confront him.

Domenicus was glad to see him. He respected him. And whether he respected him or not, he was duty-bound to obey his orders and do his bidding. But more than that, he was glad to see him because of the effect it would have on Rhodocus. So far as Domenicus was concerned, he had two scores to settle with Rhodocus. The first was official. The second was personal. He was determined to make Rhodocus regret having humiliated him at their first meeting.

"The hospitality of my father's house is yours, sir," Domenicus greeted Fortunatas and his aides. "I think you may find staying here more comfortable than at Roman headquarters."

At the evening meal, the conversation turned to news from Machaerus. "There has been much activity since you left, Domenicus. Herod and his court are in residence again. Many important people have been coming and going."

Domenicus poured wine for his guests.

"But I suppose the biggest news," Fortunatas continued, "is the beheading of John the Baptizer."

Domenicus stopped. "Beheading? Of the wilderness preacher?"

"The Lady Herodias finally got her way," Fortunatas said, swirling the wine in his cup.

"He hardly seemed worth it," said Domenicus.

Fortunatas looked at him oddly.

One of the aides, Marcus, spoke up. "Oh, he was worth it. He insulted the lady with all his talk about the sins of her divorce and remarriage to Herod."

"I was ordered to witness the gory affair," Justinius grimaced. "She tricked Herod into ordering the beheading."

Domenicus sat down. "This news will affect Jesus."

"Jesus?" Fortunatas asked. "Who's that?"

"Another heretic. Like the Baptizer, this one, too, preaches that a new kingdom is at hand."

"He doesn't claim to be the Jews' Messiah, does he?"

"He is a carpenter's son," Domenicus laughed, and went on to tell them about Jesus and his father making looms and coming to set them up for Geshem.

"What kind of a kingdom does he mean?" Fortunatas asked.

"Do we need to send legionnaires?" Marcus teased.

Domenicus laughed again. "He's only a heretic braggart, even though some people consider him a healer."

A look of fresh interest crossed Fortunatas's face.

Domenicus paused, wondering at the look, and immediately regretted his words.

"Do you know anyone this Jesus has healed?" Fortunatas wanted to know.

Domenicus felt the heat of embarrassment. He had no intention of telling them his own sister was making such a ridiculous claim.

"Well—? Do you know anyone this man has healed?"

"Of course not," he said stoutly, hoping the heat of his embarrassment was not showing in his face.

"We shouldn't be bothered if he is a healer," said Justinius. "But if he is a leader of a rebellion against us, that's a different matter."

"That is curious. Neither Rhodocus nor the centurion at Capernaum has sent me a report about it." Fortunatas said, turning to Domenicus. "Add that to the list of suspicions we already have about Rhodocus."

They all raised their wine cups. With a feeling of odd expectation, Domenicus joined the salute.

Early the next morning, Domenicus led Fortunatas and his aides to Roman headquarters. No message of their visit had been sent in advance. They simply arrived, saluted the startled sentry and walked unannounced into the reception hall used by Rhodocus.

The centurion glanced up from where he was seated behind a large table, and at the sight of the three visiting officers, scrambled to his feet.

Domenicus stepped forward to make the introductions. While he could not be certain, he thought Rhodocus's face seemed to pale a bit. In his most formal manner, he said, "Centurion Rhodocus, let me present the honorable Tribune Flavius Fortunatas."

Rhodocus bowed, smiled and extended his hand in greeting.

Fortunatas stood stock still. No change of expression crossed his face.

"And these," Domenicus continued, enjoying Rhodocus's discomfort, "are the aides-de-camp to Tribune Fortunatas, Commander Lucius Marcus and Commander Alphaeus Justinius."

Again, Rhodocus attempted to greet the visitors. And once again, was rebuffed.

Domenicus reached into the folds of his tunic and brought forth the same certification parchment that Rhodocus had refused to accept from him during his first visit. "And these are my credentials as liaison officer to the tribune. You will see that they specify my duties here on these premises."

"And they also verify his authority to act in my behalf," Fortunatas said. "I am quite sure you will find them in order, won't you, Centurion Rhodocus?"

Now there was no doubt that Rhodocus's face grew pale. Domenicus enjoyed the sight, relished it, in fact, as the certification parchment was returned to him.

Fortunatas stepped away and inspected the collection of weapons displayed on the walls of the reception hall. "Do these belong to you, centurion?"

"They do."

"Why are they here?"

"Why?"

"Yes, why? We are not at war with anyone in Galilee, or in Samaria, or in Judea. We are peacekeepers, centurion. Did you not know that?"

A funny, inarticulate sound rose in Rhodocus's throat, and translated itself into a peculiar look on his face.

"I think you should have these deadly looking weapons taken down from this wall. In fact, I know they should be. I will not have them on display as long as my men and I are using this hall as our workplace."

Rhodocus's eyes bulged in surprise.

Fortunatas turned to him. "I'm sure you can find another area for your office while I remain in Magdala."

"Of course—" Rhodocus stammered.

"My men and I have accepted the gracious invitation of Liaison Domenicus to stay at his father's house. But we will need to work out of these headquarters."

"I shall have the weapons removed immediately."

"Yes, do that." Fortunatas took off his helmet, placed it on the large work table, and turned to Domenicus. "Do you still have the list of records we wish to examine?"

Domenicus retrieved a small parchment from his tunic.

"Would you mind going with Centurion Rhodocus to find those records and have him bring them here for us to work with?"

Domenicus nodded, noticing that Rhodocus appeared even more pale as they left the room to do the bidding of Tribune Flavius Fortunatas.

Kingdom of heaven? Was this the kingdom that represented a threat to the Romans and to Herod?
11

FOR MANY DAYS immediately following her healing at the hands of Jesus, Magdalene stayed in Capernaum at the house of Ephraim with her friends Susanna and Joanna. When her parents arrived, they too stayed in the house of their old friends.

Each day many other people, both friends and strangers, came to the house wanting to see the woman from whom seven demons had been cast out. Magdalene met with as many as she could, but often the number of people was overwhelming and she would have to retreat to a far part of the house.

In the evenings when Jesus and his men returned from preaching in and around Capernaum, they often came to Ephraim's to visit. It was then that the time passed in a golden haze of closeness and joy. Even James appeared to be more considerate of Susanna, and she flourished with every bit of attention he directed toward her.

"Susanna reminds me of me," Magdalene said to Joanna one evening. "That's the way I react to the attentions of Jesus."

"But Jesus loves you," Joanna replied. "And I'm still not sure about James's feelings toward Susanna."

"Is that why Jesus is so patient with my shallowness of understanding?"

"Shallowness of understanding? What do you mean?"

"I wish I understood more about what he thinks, what he believes. I don't know what kind of kingdom he talks about. Is he going to fight with the Romans? Domenicus says he is their enemy."

Joanna glanced down and twisted her fingers. "Chuza says that Herod thinks of Jesus as an enemy, too."

"And I don't really understand why he stayed up on the mountainside tonight by himself."

"Peter said he wanted to spend the night praying to God."

"That's what I mean," Magdalene said. "I don't really know this God of his, any more than I really know him. And I want to know everything about Jesus."

"I doubt you can ever fully know him, my friend." There was a note of distant warning in Joanna's voice.

Magdalene leaned toward her. "Oh, Joanna, don't you see? Neither of us has even heard him preach! The least we could do—the least I could do, especially—is to go and hear his message."

Susanna came from the house and joined them. Magdalene told her what they had been talking about.

"James and the others are going west of the city in the morning to meet Jesus when he comes down from the mountainside. Why don't we go with them? He most likely will preach before returning to the city."

"What about the crowds?" Joanna resisted. "Won't they recognize Magdalene and press about her?"

Susanna gave a small laugh. "She is much less likely to be recognized there than here."

And so it was that on the next day Magdalene, Joanna and Susanna went with Peter, James and the others outside the city to meet Jesus. He came down from the mountainside and stood on a level place. A large crowd of believers gathered, and were joined by a number of people from all over Judea, from Jerusalem, and from the coast of Tyre and Sidon. They had all come to hear him. Many had come to be healed of their diseases.

Those troubled by evil spirits were cured, and the people all tried to touch Jesus because power was coming from him and healing them all. Magdalene fell to her knees, reliving the joy of her own healing, and in her heart she sang the praises of the Hebrew God. Joanna and Susanna knelt on either side of her and lifted their hearts with praise for the healing of their long-time friend. Words of praise and thanksgiving could be heard everywhere among the people.

The crowd grew quiet and Jesus began to speak.

"Blessed are the poor in spirit, for theirs is the kingdom of heaven."

Kingdom of heaven? Magdalene repeated the phrase under her breath. Was this the kingdom that represented a threat to the Romans and to Herod? Was she now beholding what Domenicus scorned and was afraid of? She moved from her kneeling position, sat down on the ground and clutched her knees to her chest, concentrating again on what Jesus was saying.

"Blessed are those who mourn, for they shall be comforted. Blessed are the meek, for they shall inherit the earth. Blessed are those who hunger and thirst for righteousness, for they will be filled. Blessed are you when men hate you, when they exclude and insult you, and reject your name as evil because of the Son of Man."

She thought of Rhodocus and the rumors he had spread dishonoring her name. Did it really matter that he had done so when she knew the truth of it all?

"Rejoice and be glad. Great is your reward in heaven, for in the same way, they persecuted the prophets who were before you."

He spoke of spirit and of truth, Magdalene told herself. She glanced at Joanna, wondering if she, too, realized what Jesus meant. Obviously she did, for there was an expression of rapt attention on her face.

Jesus, who had been standing, now sat down to continue to speak with all those who had come. "I tell you who hear me to love your enemies. Do good to those who hate you. Bless those who curse you. Pray for those who mistreat you."

Once again, Magdalene thought of Rhodocus. He was an enemy. How could she love him? Then she thought of her brother Domenicus, who considered Jesus an enemy and who, according to her parents, refused to accept that Jesus had healed her. Could this mean that she was an enemy to her own brother?

"If you love those who love you, what credit is that to you? Even sinners love those who love them. And if you are good to those who are good to you, what credit is that to you?"

Magdalene was fascinated. Jesus seemed to be speaking to her personally.

"Love your enemies. Be good to them. Then your reward will be great. Be merciful just as your Father in heaven is merciful."

A tremor went through Magdalene. Jesus seemed to be looking directly at her.

"Do not judge and you will not be judged. Do not condemn, and you will not be condemned. Forgive and you will be forgiven. Give, and it will be given to you. A good measure, pressed down, shaken together and running over, will be poured into your lap. For with the measure you use, it will be measured to you." Jesus stood up again and raised his arms toward heaven in a gesture of surrender and praise, signaling that he had finished his teaching for the day.

Those in the crowd who had been seated rose to their feet, too. From the front of the crowd a man hurried toward Jesus and spoke with him in an animated manner. But to Magdalene's surprise, Jesus' reaction was somber rather than animated. In fact, it seemed to her that he turned away in sorrow.

Joanna and Susanna noticed it too. "What do you think the man said to him?" Susanna asked.

Magdalene shook her head and watched Jesus

turn to Peter to pass along whatever the stranger had told him. The disciples huddled around him, apparently discussing it.

"Come. Let us go back to your father's house, Susanna. If the news is something we should know, Jesus will tell us."

When they approached the house of Susanna's parents, they saw a crowd standing in the street before its gate.

"Something terrible must have happened," Susanna said.

"I wonder if it has something to do with what the man told Jesus," Joanna said.

"Susanna, go and ask someone what is wrong," Magdalene said, nudging her friend with an elbow.

Susanna went toward the crowd and spoke with a woman standing nearest the gate. In another moment, she turned and motioned for Magdalene and Joanna to come and follow her. At a back entrance to her parents' house, Susanna told them what she had learned. "John the Baptizer has been beheaded."

Magdalene felt sick. "That means that Jesus will be in danger, too, doesn't it?"

Joanna braced herself against the courtyard wall.

Upon delivering the news, Susanna's face had gone pale. She began to stammer.

"Don't try to talk," Magdalene comforted. "We all feel the same."

The back gate swung open and Jesus entered, followed by Peter and the others. A grim expression rimmed his mouth. His eyes held a sad, far-distant look that sent a chill through Magdalene. It was as if he were looking into the future, recognizing destiny and his own place in it.

She went to him. "Can I help you, my friend? Is there some way I can lift your burden?"

The distant look eased from his eyes. The line of grimness disappeared from his mouth. "Your caring comforts me."

She took his hand, led him to a nearby bench, and urged him to sit down. The others found places nearby to sit or stand. Susanna excused herself and vanished into the house. Joanna came and sat on the bench next to Magdalene.

"The death of our brother, John the Baptizer, is a message to each of you who closely follow me," Jesus said, looking at his twelve men. "There is also a message for those of you who are my friends. The message is not a kind one. It is one of danger." He paused and looked around at each person, as if he were assessing their reactions.

No one drew back. No expression changed. No one turned from him.

He sighed heavily. "Remember that you are free to make your own choice."

Still, no one moved.

Deep in her heart, Magdalene realized how totally she now cared for this man from Nazareth. And how, without her even knowing it, her life had been intertwined with his from the beginning of time. She belonged to him. And he to her. She would follow him and serve him because he gave her a sense of purpose. If, as many claimed, he really was the Messiah, then she could think of no higher calling than to help him accomplish his life's mission. Danger seemed a small price to pay for the joy of being near him.

Susanna reappeared from the house carrying a basket of fruit and cheese which she served to everyone. Two servants followed after her, serving cups of wine.

"Where did the beheading take place?" Joanna asked.

"At the Fortress Machaerus on the orders of the tetrarch, Herod Antipas."

"And my husband, Chuza? Was he involved?"

Jesus shook his head.

"You know he would not be involved," Magdalene said gently. "He could not be your husband and be involved."

"Herod Antipas is a strong man, a persuasive ruler. My husband has served him for many years." Joanna looked at Jesus. "But I am heartened that he was not involved in the death of your friend."

Jesus put down his wine cup and stood up. "Susanna, my thanks to you for your hospitality. Extend my thanks to your parents, if you will. My men and I must leave Capernaum. There is much for us to do."

Peter and the other men began getting to their feet, saying their goodbyes, and walking toward the gate.

Jesus turned to Magdalene. "Take care, my good friend, until we see each other again."

A lump came to Magdalene's throat. She fought it down, smiled and said, "I shall miss you in the days to come."

No carpenter's son
had the power to heal . . .
12

AND INDEED, IN THE DAYS to come, Magdalene did miss Jesus. She missed the evenings of camaraderie enjoyed at the house of Susanna's parents when Jesus and his men came to visit. She remembered with reverence his wisdom. She thought again and again with thanksgiving about her healing at his hands. She wished to somehow show her gratitude.

She mentioned this need to her parents and the servant girl, Ramah, during the return journey to Magdala. Joanna and her servants had left on the royal barge to go directly to Tiberias, and then on to Jerusalem to meet Chuza.

"Your feelings of wanting to express your gratitude are understandable," Hannah reassured Magdalene as they walked together, following Geshem.

Ramah trailed behind. "But I imagine that Jesus already knows how you feel."

"Perhaps. But shouldn't I be able to give him something? Or to do something for him?"

"You have a generous heart, my daughter," Hannah said. "I wish your brother was more like you."

Mildly surprised at the mention of Domenicus, Magdalene realized that as Jesus was seldom out of her mind, Domenicus was never out of her mother's mind. "I wonder if he will ever accept my healing?"

"Oh, he'll accept your healing. When he sees you, he cannot help but know that you are healed."

With a questioning look, she glanced at her mother.

"I have never seen you so beautiful," Hannah explained in a matter-of-fact tone. "You are radiant. Domenicus will think so too. He will see the healing. What he won't accept is that Jesus, a carpenter's son, is the one who healed you."

"He is now a rabbi, my mother. A man of God."

"He is the son of man," Hannah corrected.

Geshem overheard. "He is also the Son of God."

Both women hesitated.

"Didn't you hear him say it? Over and over he spoke of himself as the Son of God," Geshem reminded them, slowing his pace so they all could walk together. "Jesus claimed that he and his Father were one. He spoke of God, the Hebrew God, in a familiar way, as if he knew him as his personal father."

"Then you think he could be the Jews' Messiah?" Hannah asked. "Ephraim seemed uncertain."

"What other man do we know who can heal people?" Geshem replied. "We heard that it happened. Over and over, we heard about healings. And even though we were not present when our daughter was healed, I do not doubt that the healing took place. Over and over, when we went to hear him preach, we saw healings happen to others. What other man do we know who teaches with such authority? Who teaches of peace and fairness, of justice, and of treating your neighbor as you want your neighbor to treat you?"

"And what other man says that we should love our enemies?" Magdalene added. "To love an enemy is not easy to do."

"He is an idealist," said Hannah. "That is a fact."

"He makes us look inside ourselves to find the best of our spirits, doesn't he?" Magdalene said.

Her mother ignored the question of inner life and asked a much more practical question. "Do you think Domenicus will believe what we have learned about Jesus?"

Geshem shrugged. "Domenicus can believe what he wishes. As a man, that is his right."

"If the Tribune Fortunatas has arrived, we may not even have a chance to tell Domenicus about Jesus."

"Perhaps that's just as well," Geshem said.

The sun was very low above the western hills by the time they arrived in Magdala. The house was quiet. Hannah sent Ramah to find Tobias, while Magdalene went to the weaving room to greet the weavers and announce their return. As she crossed the courtyard she saw a man unknown to her standing in the doorway to the weaving room. She slowed her pace, wondering if it might be the Tribune Fortunatas. By his clothing, she knew he was Roman. "Can I be of service, sir?" she asked as she drew near him.

He turned in surprise.

"I am Magdalene, daughter of the house of Geshem."

The look of surprise evaporated into a smile. He bowed.

She was quite near him now and able to see his face. High cheekbones and an aquiline nose gave him a proud, almost arrogant look. His eyes, however, redeemed him from arrogance. They were deep-set, dark in color and held lights of good humor and directness.

"My name is Flavius Fortunatas," he said. "Tribune Fortunatas. Your brother is my liaison."

Magdalene gave a slight nod. "Welcome to our home, tribune."

"We—my men and I—already are enjoying your hospitality. Your brother was kind enough to billet us here rather than in the Roman headquarters. I hope that meets with your parents' approval—and with yours."

"Of course, tribune." Aware that the weavers had stopped their work to listen to the conversation, she walked away from the door and out into the courtyard.

The Roman followed her. "The trip to Capernaum for yourself and for your parents was enjoyable?"

She nodded, wondering if Domenicus had

revealed the purpose of their trip. It was unlikely, considering his general attitude toward Jesus and toward her healing. On the other hand, his scorn of the entire idea could have prompted a disclosure.

"I thought it must have been enjoyable," said Fortunatas. "You and your parents have been gone many days."

She nodded again, suspicious now of his curiosity. "You must let me introduce you to my parents. Come."

He followed her across the courtyard and into the main part of the house. "Perhaps my men and I should find other quarters now that your family has returned."

She gave no answer, feeling that it was her father's place for such a decision, and walked on into the main room where her mother was serving her father a cup of wine.

Both glanced up. At the sight of Fortunatas, Geshem rose from his chair, cordial enough but wary.

"Father and Mother," Magdalene said. "This is Flavius Fortunatas, the tribune for whom Domenicus is liaison."

Geshem's wariness dissipated. "Welcome, tribune, welcome indeed."

Fortunatas bowed to each of them.

"Come. Share the wine with me," Geshem said, motioning to a chair. Hannah poured more wine and served Fortunatas. He accepted it, raised the cup in a salute of respect to Geshem, and sat down. As Geshem sipped at his wine, he seemed perfectly at ease at having this Roman in his house. Magdalene thought of Rhodocus and how ill-at-ease her father would be with him. She wondered if Rhodocus and Fortunatas were friends.

"I hope you have found things to your liking here in Magdala, tribune," her father said.

"Indeed. Your son has helped to make this one of the more pleasant trips I have had."

"Even with Rhodocus?" Geshem asked with surprising candor.

Fortunatas laughed. "I see you know something about the Centurion Rhodocus."

"Unfortunately, yes."

"I think your son and my men and I have had a squelching effect on him in your absence."

"Really? In what way?"

"Well, for one thing, he will now be more accountable to the people of Magdala. We have seen to that."

"He has never reimbursed us for our sheep," Hannah spoke up from her chair at the side of the room, where she had begun some handwork.

Fortunatas turned. "I think he has now. Your son has a bag of coins for you. Payment from the personal funds of Centurion Rhodocus for the sheep his men stole from you."

Geshem's eyes went wide. "You mean he actually has paid for our sheep?"

Fortunatas nodded.

Hannah was on her feet, moving to get the cruet of wine and refill the cups of both the Roman and Geshem. "It is too good to be true," she said. "Too good."

"And what do you think about this, Magdalene?" Fortunatas asked. "Are you as pleased as your parents?"

She smiled. "I would be more pleased to know that he could no longer interfere with my father's leadership of the spinners and weavers."

"My daughter worries about me too much," Geshem apologized.

A thoughtful look crossed the Roman's face. "You are a fortunate man."

"We are a fortunate family," Hannah said, returning to her place and picking up her handwork again. "And Magdalene is the most fortunate of all."

"Oh? In what way?"

"She has just recently been healed of a terrible, and lifelong, affliction."

Embarrassed by her mother's candor, Magdalene failed to notice how quickly the Roman straightened in his chair, and with what fresh interest he stared at her.

"My dear wife," Geshem said, "the tribune is not interested in the state of Magdalene's health."

"Oh, but I am."

Together, they turned toward him in surprise.

Fortunatas set down his wine cup and leaned forward intently. "Tell me about this healing, Magdalene."

She hesitated for the longest of moments, wondering if it was a trick, yet seeing nothing but a surprised earnestness in his face. It was a look that mirrored her own feelings when she first had learned that Jesus could heal, and she realized that Fortunatas, too, might have a personal need for healing. Haltingly she began, searching for the right words that would describe the heaviness and fear she had carried all her life because of the strange spells. Her words came easier as she began to tell of how she learned about Jesus healing people of all kinds of illnesses and diseases.

She even realized that it wouldn't matter if the Roman did not believe her. She knew it was true. She knew healings happened. Jesus healed. He had healed *her!*

The expression of rapt attention remained on his face.

She grew more confident. The words now flowed through her as a fresh spring bubbles from the earth. She spoke of seeking out Jesus, of asking him to heal her. By the time she was telling about the healing itself, her mind and heart were soaring afresh with the joy of it all. And when she finished the story of her miracle, a breathless quiet of wonderful mystery filled the room and held them all suspended in its simplicity and its truth.

A shuffle of feet came from the doorway.

Magdalene slowly turned.

Domenicus stood just inside the room, a stricken look on his face. Behind him were two other Romans, eyes wide, mouths agape at what they had heard; and more importantly, at what they saw in their tribune's attentive face.

Justinius cleared his throat and moved around Domenicus to come and introduce himself to Geshem. Marcus followed.

Fortunatas stood up. "Domenicus, why didn't you tell me of this miracle that has happened to your sister?"

"We—uh—we had more pressing matters to attend," Domenicus stammered. "It never occurred to me that—"

"But we talked about this Jesus."

"You said you knew him," Marcus said. "That he was a carpenter's son. That he made looms."

"You also told us he was a braggart," Justinius said.

"And a heretic," Fortunatas added.

"Why did you say such things about our friend Jesus?" Geshem asked his son.

Domenicus looked at his father, speechless.

Geshem stood, went to Domenicus and searched his face. "Were you afraid that your Roman friends would think you were Jewish, too, my son?"

Domenicus reddened.

A new, strained stillness filtered through the room.

Geshem shook his head and walked away.

Domenicus suddenly found his voice. "This talk of healing, it's a fable! You're grown people! You are Romans, we are Greeks. How can any of you believe such a fable?"

Magdalene went to him. "Please, my brother, my healing is real. Can you not be happy for me even in that?"

He backed away from her.

"Jesus is our friend," she pursued. "He has been for many years."

"I told you once before, he is no longer our friend," Domenicus said recklessly. "He talks of establishing a new kingdom. He is an enemy of Rome."

A cry of anguish went up from Hannah.

Geshem paled.

Marcus and Justinius exchanged looks of surprise.

Fortunatas walked to the cruet of wine and poured cups for each of his men. "You told us earlier that we didn't need to worry about that. But if what you are now telling us is true, Domenicus . . . "

"Why should I lie?" He strode to the table and poured a cup of wine for himself.

"Why should your sister lie?" Hannah snapped.

Domenicus ignored her and turned instead to Fortunatas. "You must excuse us, tribune. This family matter need not be aired in front of you."

Fortunatas hesitated, looking toward Magdalene as if for a signal to stay. When she gave none, he put down the wine cruet and nodded curtly for his men to follow him out into the courtyard.

As their guests disappeared, Hannah stepped toward Domenicus. "I ask you again why you think your sister would lie? Especially about such an important thing?"

"My mother, you don't understand."

"Are you saying because she is a woman she has no sense?" Magdalene challenged mockingly. "And because I am only a woman, I cannot possibly understand, either?"

Anger flared red in Domenicus's face. He turned to Geshem. "Tell her to be quiet. My whole future may be at stake over this impossible subject."

Geshem drew himself up to his full height. "Your future? Is your future so important that you have let rudeness violate the hospitality of this house?"

"Rudeness? I am not the one claiming healing from a heretic!" Domenicus shouted. "I didn't begin talking about such a foolish subject."

"You are quite right," Geshem said. "You didn't begin talking about it. Your mother brought it up first. And then your friend Fortunatas asked Magdalene to tell him about it."

"Fortunatas—?"

Geshem nodded. "Fortunatas seemed very interested, almost as if he had a personal reason for wanting to know all about Jesus and his healing powers. You are not only a disbeliever, you are a rude host. You owe your Roman friends an apology."

"And what is more," Hannah added, "you owe your sister an even greater apology."

Domenicus looked stunned, dumbfounded.

Hannah turned away from him, took Magdalene by the arm and led her from the room. Geshem followed, leaving Domenicus to repair the breach of hospitality with the Romans as best he could.

For several seconds more, he stared after them without moving, disbelief holding him anchored. He expected his father to be on Magdalene's side. He always was. But the fact that his mother took her side shocked him, made him wonder for the merest second if he might be wrong about Jesus. Then logic returned. No carpenter's son had the power to heal.

He straightened, looked down and realized he was still holding the cup of wine. He drank it all in one gulp and walked out into the courtyard.

Fortunatas was seated on a bench. Marcus and Justinius stood nearby.

"I apologize, my friends," he said, trying to sound lighthearted. "Family arguments can be embarrassing. But all is well now."

Marcus and Justinius glanced at each other.

Fortunatas stood up. "I think it will be best if we go to the garrison headquarters for the night."

"Please don't," Domenicus said. "If you move out now, I shall never again be able to face my family. My father is very strict about his rules of hospitality. Please. To save my face, you must stay."

Fortunatas inspected the young man through stern eyes, and slowly shook his head. "Garrison headquarters is where we need to be now. Have your servants bring our gear to us there."

His father gave him a hard look.
"The Romans pay you, don't they?"
13

MAGDALENE LAY AWAKE that night thinking about this new confrontation with her brother. Her heart was burdened, upset and uncertain, over what she could do about his enmity toward Jesus.

But something else bothered her, too. Why was the Roman, Fortunatas, so interested in hearing about the experience of her healing? She wished she could talk more with him, and regretted that he and his men had not continued as guests in her father's house.

She wished that Jesus were here. He would know what to do.

When she awoke the next morning, her heart was still troubled and her mind still filled with curiosity. She got up, washed her face and hands at a small basin which a servant had filled with water the night before, dressed in a fresh tunic and robe, and combed her hair.

"Magdalene?" her mother called out, coming into the sleeping alcove. "You have a visitor."

"Who?"

"Tribune Fortunatas."

"Where is Domenicus?"

"Who can say? Your father thinks he did not sleep here at all."

Magdalene went to a small chest, picked out a corded sash, tied it about her waist, and turned to her mother. "I wish he could believe I am healed. And I wish—"

"You wish he believed in Jesus?"

She nodded, and gave a heavy sigh.

"Come along," her mother urged. "The Roman is waiting for you in the courtyard. I had refreshments taken out to him."

"You won't be with me?"

Hannah shook her head. "He came to see you, my daughter."

The day was bright with early sun. The merest breeze touched the hibiscus, and beyond, oleanders swayed in a delicate dance of color. Shielding her eyes against the brightness, she stepped out into the courtyard.

Fortunatas came to greet her. "I apologize for coming so early, but I have been ordered to Jerusalem. And I wanted to see you before I left."

"Jerusalem? My friend Joanna is there."

"Joanna?"

"Yes, she was with me when I was healed."

A look of fresh interest crossed his face. "Then she is a Jesus-believer, too?"

Magdalene hesitated.

Fortunatas pressed the answer. "How could she not be, if she was with you when you received your healing?"

"That is not why I hesitated," Magdalene explained. "I wouldn't want to put Joanna in danger."

"Danger?"

"She is the wife of Chuza, minister to Herod Antipas."

The Roman's eyebrows arched upward in surprise and understanding. "Yes—discretion would be advisable."

Magdalene appreciated his sensitivity, and felt bold enough to ask the reason for his interest in Jesus and healing. "And would discretion be needed in your case too?"

He smiled and led her to the wooden bench near the courtyard wall. "Am I that transparent?"

She gave a small shrug. "Jesus is obviously of interest to you. Is it because he is so controversial?"

"That is part of it, I suppose. But he is also obviously a very different kind of man. I know of no other who can heal. Physicians help with their herbs and medicines, but . . . " His voice trailed off, and a look of sadness filled his eyes.

Sympathy welled up inside Magdalene. Her immediate instinct was to question him; to ask if someone dear to him suffered an illness or if he himself had need of healing. But a second thought made her realize that to ask any question might deepen his sense of sadness. She glanced about the courtyard, wondering what she could say that would help him. And then she remembered something Peter had told her about Jesus. "I recall an incident of healing where the person in need of the healing was not even in the presence of Jesus."

Despite the sadness, he looked attentive—as though she had hinted at the solution to a lingering concern of his. "Peter, one of Jesus' disciples, told me of a Roman soldier like yourself who had a servant who was paralyzed and in terrible suffering. The soldier came to Jesus and told him of the situation. Jesus said that he would go to the servant. But the centurion replied that he didn't feel worthy to have Jesus come under his roof. 'Just say the word, and my servant will be healed,' he told Jesus. 'For I myself am a man under authority with soldiers under me; and when I tell them to do something, they do it. And when I tell my servant to do something, he does it.'

"Peter told me Jesus was astonished—he said to Peter and the others that he had not found anyone in Israel with such great faith. And to the centurion he said, 'Go! It will be done, just as you believed it would.' And the servant was healed at that very hour."

A strange new light had come onto Fortunatas's face during the telling of the miracle. And when Magdalene finished, he smiled. "By the heavens, I must meet this Jesus of Nazareth."

"He is easily found near Capernaum. Can you go there before going to Jerusalem?"

"I think not. My orders are to proceed to Jerusalem at once. But perhaps in a few days I can come back to Capernaum to find him. At least, I shall try." He smiled at her. "You make a fine witness for him. He must consider it wonderful support. Thank you for sharing what you know of Jesus with me." He stood to leave. "Will you thank your parents for me again? My men and I appreciate the hospitality of this house. Very much."

"Will Domenicus be going with you to Jerusalem?" Magdalene asked, walking with him to the gate.

He looked at her in surprise. "Didn't he come back here last night and tell your parents that he would be leaving?"

"I think not."

"He will be traveling with me and my men. We have almost finished our work here, and I will need him with me in Jerusalem."

Magdalene felt a mixture of emotions at this news.

"I, too, am sorry he doesn't believe in Jesus," Fortunatas continued, as if reading her mind. "He is still recklessly young. Life has not touched him hard yet."

Once again, Magdalene appreciated Fortunatas's sensitivity. He smiled at her, gave a salute of farewell, and disappeared through the gate. She glanced away, not knowing what to say. As she closed the gate behind him, she leaned against it, deep in thought. She was glad Domenicus would be going away. She was glad he would be with a man like Fortunatas. Maybe the tribune could influence him in some way that would settle his recklessness. But the idea of Domenicus being in Jerusalem worried her, too. She hoped he would not try to impose himself on Joanna's hospitality; and beyond that, she prayed he would be discreet about Joanna's feelings toward Jesus.

She went on into the house, walked through it and out into the back courtyard. In its measured climb through the heavens, the sun had pushed away all the shade of early morning, leaving the courtyard vulnerable to a growing brightness and warmth. Magdalene welcomed it. She sat down on a wooden bench near the weaving room, still thinking about Fortunatas and still regretting last night's argument with Domenicus.

It was unthinkable that he would leave Magdala without telling his parents goodbye. Disapproving as he might be of her and her friendship with Jesus, and as disbelieving as he might be of her healing, he owed his mother and father the courtesy of a decent farewell. It was an obligation of gratitude, she told herself; an obligation of gratitude as deep as the one she owed to Jesus.

The remembrance of her own obligation caused her to straighten. In the upset of last night's argument, the need to show Jesus her gratitude had been forgotten. Now it was something to consider. She rose from the bench and paced back and forth across the courtyard thinking about it, reliving her new-found joy of freedom from fear, re-experiencing the lightness of good health and the wonderful peace deep in her soul. If only it could be that way for everyone, she thought.

Fortunatas's words came back to her: *You make a fine witness. He must consider it wonderful support. Thank you for sharing what you know of Jesus with me.*

Witness. Support. Sharing.

Jesus.

She returned to the bench and sat down, overwhelmed by new thoughts flooding into her mind. Jesus and his men did need support. They needed the support of those who had received healing; those who believed that Jesus had extraordinary powers; those who knew that he was more than mere man and that the kingdom he proclaimed had nothing to do with armies and wars but rather with the human spirit.

The kind of support they needed was in bearing witness. But there were other needs, too. Practical needs. Food, clothing for the poor who now followed Jesus, shelters, even money for the beggars. Those were things she had. All of these she could provide in support of him and his teaching! They were things he needed, and things he could accept from her. She would follow him. For as often and for as long as she could, she would follow him.

This would be her gift to him, an acknowledgment from her heart of the wondrous healing of body, mind and spirit with which he had blessed her. Excitement leapt into her mind at the idea. She would ask Joanna and Susanna to go with her as followers and helpers of Jesus. No doubt they would. Susanna would want to be near James. Like herself, Joanna would want to be near Jesus and learn more about his kingdom. And she felt sure that both Susanna and Joanna would want to help support Jesus out of their own means.

She got up from the bench and started toward the house to tell her parents of her plan, to ask their blessings for it. Before she reached the house, however, Domenicus came though a side gate.

"Oh, Domenicus, I'm so glad you have come."

At the sight of her, he abruptly stopped. A scornful look crossed his face. He brushed past her without speaking and entered the house, calling out for their parents.

Hannah appeared from the cooking area carrying a basket of bread and cheese. A servant followed her with a basket of fruit and a cruet of goat's milk.

"Is my father here?"

Hannah shook her head. "He is gone into the fields with the shepherds to check on the sheep."

Domenicus reached into his tunic and withdrew a leather pouch filled with coins. "This is from the Centurion Rhodocus. It is repayment for the sheep that were stolen some time ago."

Hannah accepted the pouch. "Tribune Fortunatas told us we could expect this. Thank you, Domenicus." She laid the pouch on the table and set the basket of bread and cheese next to it. "Your sister has not yet broken fast this morning. Would you like something to eat, too?"

He shook his head. "I have come only to gather my belongings and say farewell. Fortunatas has been ordered to Jerusalem. He is taking me with him."

Hannah turned, a look of surprise on her face. Magdalene expected her to protest. Instead, her mother's look of surprise melted into one of resignation. "I will send a servant for your father," Hannah said, going away to another part of the house.

Before Hannah was completely out of sight, Domenicus left to gather his belongings. In fact, he hurried from the room—as if to stay alone with Magdalene was, at the least, uncomfortable, and at the most, dangerous.

She felt disappointed. As she walked to the doorway and stared out into the sunlit courtyard, the words she had heard Jesus speak on the mountainside came back to her. *Love your enemies. Do good to them that despise you. If your brother asks you to walk a mile with him, walk with him two.* But her brother wanted nothing to do with her. Because Jesus was her friend, Domenicus chose to be her enemy.

She turned back into the room. Her mother had returned with her father more quickly than she had expected. From the other part of the house, Magdalene could hear Domenicus returning, too, the tread of his Roman boots heavy on the tile passageway.

He was carrying a satchel of his belongings. At the sight of Geshem, he made a slight bow. "Fortunatas wants me to—"

"Yes, yes," Geshem cut in. "Your mother has told me."

"Well, I—uh—I'm going to Jerusalem. It's quite an honor, really."

"So it would appear."

Domenicus shifted the satchel from one hand to the other, and glanced toward the table where the money pouch and the food baskets were.

"You've changed your mind?" Hannah asked, misinterpreting his look. "You want to take some food with you?"

He shook his head. "I want to take the money with me. Since I'm going to Jerusalem, it will be very helpful."

His father gave him a hard look. "The Romans pay you, don't they?"

Domenicus nodded.

"And they feed you and house you, do they not?"

Again Domenicus nodded, but redness began to rise in his face. He cleared his throat.

"You have no need of this money, Domenicus. None at all that I can see," his father said, walking toward the outer door. "I wish you a safe journey, as do your mother and sister. And we bid you farewell."

For a long moment, Domenicus appeared unable to move. No one else moved, either. Then Domenicus uttered a swearing sound, wheeled about and left.

Dejected, Magdalene's mother sat down on the bench near the table. Geshem went to her, sat beside her and put his arm around her shoulders. "It is just as well, my wife. Just as well."

Feeling a strange mixture of sadness and relief, Magdalene went to them and hugged them both. "I am sorry, my parents. Truly sorry that my healing and my friendship with Jesus have caused Domenicus to feel so much dislike."

Her mother patted her hand. "It is not your fault, Magdalene. Domenicus has hardened his heart against what he does not understand."

"It is his ambition that bothers me," Geshem said, examining the money pouch. "It's like a sickness."

"We must still love him," Magdalene said. She moved to the far side of the table and poured a cup of goat's milk for herself. "It is what Jesus would tell us to do."

"He would pray for Domenicus, too, wouldn't he?" Hannah asked, a faraway tone in her voice.

"Well," Magdalene said, "he does teach that we are to love our enemies, to 'pray for those who despitefully use you.' I regret to say that this may now include Domenicus."

They stayed quiet for a time, heeding their own thoughts. Then her mother turned toward her and changed the subject. "Have you given any more thought to what we talked about on the way home from Capernaum?"

"You mean about how I might thank Jesus for my healing?"

Hannah nodded.

"Yes, I have."

"And—"? Geshem asked. "What have you decided?"

Magdalene put her cup down, came around the table and sat beside them. "I want to help his ministry. I want to bear witness to what he says and does." She paused, trying to measure her parents' reactions, uncertain of their thoughts from the expressions on their faces. "I want to help him," she continued. "I want to learn from him. But more than anything, I want to be with him."

"You mean travel around the countryside with him?" her father asked.

She nodded.

"But my daughter, you are a single woman," her mother objected. "What will people say?"

"If Joanna and Susanna will go with me, what could people say?"

Geshem looked startled. "Joanna? But what about her husband?"

"And what about Susanna's parents?" Hannah asked with an arched eyebrow. "Ephraim will never allow such a thing."

"It is all a matter of trust, my parents," Magdalene said carefully. "A matter of trust, and in my case, a matter of obligation. I have received a very great blessing. I must witness for Jesus and the power of the Hebrew God."

Her father got up, walked to the doorway and stood looking out into the courtyard, considering her words.

Magdalene waited. She knew in her heart that her decision was the right one; she hoped her parents would decide so, too.

Geshem turned and strolled back to the table thoughtfully. He picked up the money pouch Domenicus had brought and hefted it to feel its weight. "You will need this," he said, handing it to her, "for your travels with Jesus."

He had been right all along.
Jesus was a heretic.
He was Rome's enemy.

14

AWE.

This was the only word Domenicus could think of to describe his feelings at the first sight of Jerusalem. From the crest of the Mount of Olives, the city shimmered in a noonday sun as bright as the gold on the great Temple of the Jews, and proscribed in his mind the wealth of the ages. The Temple was built by Herod the Great for the Jews on the site, it was said, of Solomon's own temple. Wealth. Everywhere, wealth.

From the floor of the Kidron Valley, the great walls of the city towered above him in a display of power that wrenched at him. He stared up at the great walls and rode in silence, unmindful of the heat, uncaring that crowds of people thronged the roadway leading up to the Sheep's Gate in the eastern wall, undisturbed that the pace of their horses was slowed almost to a standstill at the gate itself.

Once inside the gate, the roadway split into three streets. One to the left led to the Sheep Market. One to the right meandered through a throng of poor houses toward the Damascus Gate Road. The third street went in a generally straight direction toward the Fortress Antonia. Atop its massive tower, sun glinted from the helmets of legionnaires patrolling there. More power.

Wealth and power, Domenicus thought. That was what counted in life. Nothing more. And thanks to Fortunatas, he was being led into the midst of both here in Jerusalem.

He kicked at his horse, urging it to follow Fortunatas, Marcus and Justinius along the crowded street. People gave way reluctantly. Some cat-called as they passed. Others cursed. Still others spat at them. Anger bit at Domenicus. He gripped the riding crop tightly, ready to strike back.

Fortunatas turned into a different street in front of Fortress Antonia and led them across the Viaduct, a stone and wooden span connecting the Upper City with the fortress and the Temple Mount. To the left, Domenicus looked down on the houses of the Lower City clinging in precarious fashion to the sides of the Cheesemaker's Valley.

Justinius, riding just in front of him, turned in his saddle and pointed to an imposing structure on the east shoulder of the valley. "Hippodrome! There will be plenty of amusement for us here."

Domenicus nodded to an enormous building just in front of them. "And what is that?"

Justinius glanced around, then laughed. "Home!"

"Home?"

Justinius nodded. "The Hasmonean Palace. It is Pilate's headquarters in Jerusalem."

"And we will be billeted there?"

Justinius nodded again.

Domenicus felt a heady sense of elation. Wealth and power were all around him. And he was part of it! He would live in a palace, most likely eat the best food, be with men he respected and liked. And more than that, he reminded himself, he would meet people of real power and wealth. Joanna would see to that. His elation grew, bringing with it a sense of satisfaction which lasted throughout the first days of his stay in Jerusalem.

He made himself as useful to Fortunatas as he possibly could, and was rewarded with the extraordinary privilege of accompanying the tribune wherever he went during their first weeks in Jerusalem. Marcus and Justinius were assigned specific headquarters duties. But since Domenicus spoke both Aramaic and Hebrew, as well as Greek and Latin, Fortunatas found him useful in many differing situations.

He accompanied Fortunatas on a visit to the Jews' high priest, Caiaphas, to discuss the matter of setting out special sentries to keep legionnaires out of the Court of the Gentiles on the Temple Mount. They dressed in the flowing robes of pilgrims and went to the Temple Mount to see for themselves how many sentries might be needed and where they should be stationed. They inspected the Chamber of Hewn Stone where the Sanhedrin met to debate and legislate the Jewish laws. And they observed the number and demeanor of the Temple guards.

They inspected certain shops whose owners had complained of thievery and bullying by Roman soldiers, and set in motion plans to catch the guilty and punish them. They conferred with local officials about curfews in certain sections of the city, and detailed extra guards to discourage pickpockets at Hippodrome events.

In fact, Fortunatas kept Domenicus so busy that it was several weeks before he had the time to slip away to the palace of Herod Antipas to find Joanna.

His credentials as a liaison to Fortunatas got him through the sentries at the outer gates. A palace guard escorted him to Chuza's office and went away to announce him, leaving him alone in the large, well-furnished room. He glanced about, calculating Chuza's importance, considering himself lucky to know the wife of such a powerful man, and trying to remember what Chuza looked like. The only time he had met him was at Joanna's wedding. That had been many years before. He wasn't sure he would recognize Chuza.

But when a side door swung open and a short, round man came striding into the room, he knew it had to be Chuza. An old memory surfaced. The family had all teased Joanna about marrying a man of such short stature. This had to be Chuza. Domenicus bowed and raised his arm in a Roman salute.

Chuza responded with a brief nod, and eyed him with cautious interest.

"Forgive the unexpected intrusion, sir," Domenicus said in his most formal manner, realizing that Chuza did not remember him. "My name is Domenicus. I am liaison to the Tribune Fortunatas of Pontius Pilate's Headquarters Garrison."

Chuza's expression did not change, except for the merest flicker in his eyes. "You have come on official business?"

Domenicus shook his head. "I have come to see an old friend. The Lady Joanna."

Chuza's expression changed to open wariness.

"I am Domenicus of the house of Geshem in Magdala. I am brother to Magdalene." Domenicus waited, expecting some warmth of recognition. When it did not come, he began to feel like an intruder, and regretted that he had not sent a note of introduction ahead of this visit to the palace. "I only recently came to Jerusalem. And I—uh—I came to pay my respects to Joanna. And, to you, sir."

Chuza continued to carefully watch him. "My wife is not in Jerusalem at this time. But in my next communication with her, I will tell her you called."

In both word and tone, the dismissal was clear. Domenicus felt the color rise in his face as Chuza pulled a small bell from the folds of his ample tunic and jingled it in his hand. Within a matter of seconds, a palace guard appeared. "Our guest is ready to leave. Help him find his way out."

Domenicus choked back his anger, gave a curt nod to Chuza and followed the guard out of the palace. When he was back in the street, he vented his anger with an oath, and spat on the wide paving stones. He felt totally humiliated. Chuza had acted as if he had never heard of him, or of Magdalene!

Magdalene! Of course! Most likely she was the cause of such a reception. Magdalene and her healing! Magdalene and her friendship with a Jewish rabble-rouser! No wonder Chuza had acted like he didn't know anything about the house of Geshem. He spat again and walked on along the street toward the Agora.

Once he reached the Upper City's great market place, he sought out the shopkeeper who sold balsam rum, bought a small quantity and sat down on a nearby bench to sip at it and salve his bruised ego. The Agora was crowded with shoppers. Merchants and shopkeepers hawked their wares and joked with each other, haggled with buyers, and chased away little boys bent on stealing. Between the shops and the booths filled with merchandise, men squatted on their heels in groups of three or four and filled the afternoon with talk of Herod's latest tax increase, of Roman strictness for peace in the streets, of the Sanhedrin's endless debates and . . . of a Nazarene named Jesus who could heal and who was going to bring about a new kingdom.

Domenicus hesitated, his rum poised mid-air, and turned to look at the men talking about Jesus.

There were four of them, all about his own age, and they were speaking in Hebrew. "They'll get him," one of them said. "Sooner or later, the Pharisees will demand that he be imprisoned."

"I hear that Herod thinks he is John the Baptist come back to life to haunt him."

All of them laughed.

"Serves Herod right."

"What kind of kingdom is Jesus talking about?" asked another. "I hear he has only twelve men."

"That's no army. And he would need an army to bring in a new kingdom against Herod."

"And what about the Romans?" asked the first man. "They've annihilated the best armies in the world."

A fifth man joined the group then and announced, "Caiaphas is calling a special session of the Sanhedrin. We need to go quickly."

"What's this special session all about?"

"Another tax increase. Come on."

The men all got to their feet and moved off across the Agora in the direction of the Viaduct and the Temple Mount.

Domenicus regretted that the talk about Jesus had been interrupted. He wondered if Fortunatas and the others had heard such talk. They wouldn't tell him if they had. Jesus was a subject that none of them discussed with him. He would have to find out for himself just how widespread the opposition to Jesus really was. But one thing was certain: He had been right all along. Jesus was a heretic. He was Rome's enemy.

He finished the last of his rum, wondering how he could help to prove it. If he could find a way, he could be a young hero to Rome. There would come a time when Chuza would not be so quick to be rid of him.

Jesus' warning, his prophetic words about his own future, seemed to have escaped his disciples . . .
15

FOR WEEKS, JESUS had been traveling about from one town and village to another proclaiming the good news of the kingdom of God. The twelve were with him, and also some women who had been cured of evil spirits and disease. These women were helping to support Jesus and his men out of their own means.

Once Magdalene had received her parents' blessings, she had written to Joanna and Susanna, told them of her plan to travel with Jesus, and invited them to join her. Both accepted. From that time on, they were regular supporters of Jesus and his cause. Other women joined them, too. Jesus' mother, Mary, and Salome, the mother of James and John, were among them from time to time along with several others.

Often, Joanna could join them for only a few days

at a time because of Chuza's need for her to be discreet. "He is tolerant beyond what you might imagine," she told Magdalene. "And he thinks your healing is wonderful. But he cannot accept the divinity of Jesus as you and I do."

"Herod would not like him to accept it, either," Magdalene responded in her practical manner.

"That is true," Joanna agreed, and then, with a wistful look, nodded. "But someday, Chuza may believe. And when he does, he will find a way to keep it carefully to himself."

Susanna's travels with them were sometimes only for short periods as well. Her mother and father often had need of her in Capernaum, and she received no encouragement from James to be a regular supporter.

"I am growing disillusioned with James," she confided to Magdalene and Joanna one day as the group settled for a midday rest. "He is really not the man I thought he was. He is so ambitious. His whole family is!"

Magdalene exchanged a quick look with Joanna. "Why do you now think this?"

"Something I overheard."

"Overheard?"

Susanna nodded, an almost tearful look invading her face.

"What did you overhear?"

"I overheard an argument among the twelve as to which of them would be the greatest. Peter and James especially were arguing with each other. As if knowing their thoughts, Jesus took the hand of a little child who was in the crowd and had him stand beside him. Then he said to Peter and the others, 'Whoever welcomes this little child in my name welcomes me; and whoever welcomes me welcomes the one who sent me. For he who is least among you all, he is the greatest."

"And what did Peter and James say to that?" Magdalene wanted to know.

"Peter looked embarrassed."

"And James?"

"James turned away angry, and went off to where his mother Salome was sitting with Jesus' mother. Later on, Salome saw that Jesus was sitting apart from the rest. She motioned for James and John to follow, then she went to Jesus and said to him, 'I ask a favor of you, my nephew.'

"'What favor do you ask?' Jesus said.

"'Grant that these, my two sons, may sit, the one on your right hand, and the other on your left in your kingdom.'"

"And how did Jesus answer her?" Magdalene wanted to know.

"He told her she didn't know what she was asking. And then he turned to James and John and asked them if they were able to drink from the same cup he would drink from."

A feeling of wariness crept through Magdalene. "And of course, they said they could?"

"Yes, they did. But how did you know?" Susanna asked, looking puzzled, and turning to Joanna. "Did she overhear this, too?"

Joanna shook her head. "No, she didn't overhear.

But it is very easy to observe the ambition in James and John. You even have said so before."

"Go on, Susanna," Magdalene urged. "What else did Jesus tell these ambitious cousins of his?"

"He told them that whoever sat on his right hand or his left would be decided by his Father."

Magdalene leaned back on her elbows. "So that's it!"

"What's it?" Susanna blurted.

"The other ten must have overheard this same conversation. They have shown indignance toward James and John ever since Salome and Jesus' mother returned to Capernaum. The twelve have acted like the ten and the two. They have been separated like warring camps." She stood up suddenly. "That's no way for them to act. Let's take water to them. Maybe that will soothe their tempers."

"Maybe we shouldn't interfere," Susanna resisted.

"Oh, come on," Joanna said. "There is enough strife in the world without Jesus' men fighting among themselves."

Magdalene led the way down the hillside, picked up a water juglet and went to Peter and began serving the water. Joanna was right behind her. Susanna trailed. Soon all the twelve were served. Magdalene turned and saw Jesus coming from the shore of the lake. She went to him to offer water, and he took the juglet and drank from it.

"Peter and the others seem indignant. Is there a reason?" she asked him.

He glanced around her toward the men. "Yes, there is a reason." He handed the juglet back to her.

"Can I be of help?"

He smiled. "The water you have brought has cooled tempers. But the words that must be said to them are words which I must say." He turned toward the men, called them to him, and when they stood clustered about, he began. "You know that the rulers of the Gentiles lord it over them, and their high officials exercise authority over them. It is not so with you." He paused, looking at each man for a soul-searing moment.

Peter turned his face away, as if not wanting Jesus to see the resentful look in his eyes. Matthew, Thomas and Andrew looked briefly at each other. The others studied the ground.

Jesus continued. "Instead, whoever wants to become great among you must be your servant."

James and John exchanged a look of disappointment.

"And whoever wants to be first must be your slave, just as the Son of Man did not come to be served, but to serve." Jesus paused again, as if to emphasize the rest of his words, " . . . and to give his life as a ransom for many."

Magdalene felt her heart grow cold. She stared at Jesus, uncertain she had heard him correctly. He was speaking of himself. He was speaking of his own life. And of his own death. A ransom? A shiver of fear went through her. She had not thought of death where Jesus was concerned. She did not like thinking of it now. And yet she knew he had enemies. Beginning with her own brother, she already had learned that awful truth. Why had she not connected such enmity with the idea of danger and death?

She glanced at the twelve. Had they who were closest to him not realized it either?

Obviously they had not. Their attention seemed focused on ambitions and jealousies which were all too human. Jesus' warning, his prophetic words about his own future, seemed to have escaped them. Wondering if this was the first time he had spoken of his future to the twelve, Magdalene searched Jesus' face and marvelled that there was no sign of fear in it.

He spoke again. "Let us now return to Capernaum for the night. Tomorrow we will make our way to the Plain of Gennesaret, and after that, perhaps to Phoenicia. There is much teaching and healing to be done, and time grows short."

For the next several weeks Jesus and the twelve stayed in the vicinity of the Plain of Gennesaret, and often came into Magdala itself. Geshem and Hannah were delighted to have Magdalene home once more and opened their house as a headquarters for Jesus and his men. Susanna had stayed in Capernaum. Joanna returned to Jerusalem, feeling that she had been away from Chuza too long.

Geshem, Hannah and Magdalene told all the people they knew that Jesus had returned, and they spread the word into the surrounding country. People came from every direction to hear his teachings. They brought with them their sick and begged Jesus to let the sick just touch the edge of his cloak. All who touched him were healed.

One late afternoon after Jesus and the twelve returned to Geshem's house and were taking refreshments in the back courtyard, some Pharisees and teachers of the law came from Jerusalem to see him.

"Do you wish to see them?" Magdalene asked when Tobias brought the message that they were at the gate.

He nodded. "But I will go out to them. There is no need to further impose on the hospitality of this house." He started to stand.

Magdalene put a restraining hand on his arm. "You honor our house. You know that. Besides, you look tired. You have healed so many today. Let me bring these men in to you."

With a smile of gratitude, Jesus sat back down.

Geshem chuckled. "I keep telling you, Jesus, a thoughtful woman is a blessing beyond all."

Motioning for Tobias to come with her, Magdalene left to bring in the visitors. There were four of them. By their dress, they were obviously men of means, and they acted surprised that it was a woman who invited them to come in.

The tallest of the four seemed to be their spokesman. He introduced himself as Hedadiah. "My friends and I are seeking the Nazarene. We are told he is staying here."

"That is true," Magdalene said with a slight nod of her head. "My father's house welcomes you. Follow me. I will take you to Jesus."

As they entered the back courtyard, Geshem stood to greet them, then introduced Jesus and the twelve. The men bowed and seated themselves on a nearby bench that Magdalene indicated.

Jesus observed them carefully.

"We have come to see you, Nazarene," said Hedadiah, "because of rumors we have been hearing."

"What kind of rumors?"

"One rumor is that you claim to be a rabbi."

Jesus' look did not waver.

"Another rumor concerns your disciples' behavior. It is said that they don't wash their hands before they eat. Why do they break the tradition of the elders?"

"And why do you break the command of God for the sake of your tradition?" Jesus asked.

The four visitors looked surprised and glanced at each other.

"God said, 'Honor your father and mother.' But you say that if a man says to his father or mother, 'Whatever help you might otherwise have received from me is a gift devoted to God,' he is not to honor his father with it. Thus, you nullify the word of God for the sake of your tradition. You hypocrites!"

Hedadiah's face reddened. The others sat with mouths hanging open.

The twelve shuffled about, looking uncomfortable. Though Jesus' tone held no animosity, his words were harsh, their meaning blunt. "Isaiah was right when he prophesied about you," he went on. "Isaiah said there were people like you who pay honor with their lips but whose hearts are far from me. He also said there are people like you who worship me in vain, and whose teachings are but the rules taught by men."

Hedadiah quickly rose to his feet. The other three stood up, too. "We are men of learning, sir," Hedadiah said. "And you are speaking blasphemy. For you speak as if you, yourself, were God."

Magdalene held her breath. A chill of fear raced through her at the looks of resentment on the faces of the visitors.

"Take it as you will, men of learning," Jesus said without rancor. "But I ask you to listen and understand. What goes into a man's mouth, even unwashed hands, does not make him unclean. But what comes out of his mouth does make him unclean."

Hedadiah looked at Magdalene and Geshem. "We will take leave of your house," he said, bowing. The other three followed his lead.

Magdalene moved forward. "I will show you the way out."

By the time she returned, the twelve were all talking at once among themselves. Then Peter turned to Jesus and said, "Don't you know that the Pharisees were offended by your words?"

Jesus met his accusation with a level gaze. "Leave them. They are blind guides. If a blind man leads a blind man, both will fall into a pit."

Peter shook his head in confusion. "Explain the parable to us."

"Are you still so dull?" Jesus asked with a sigh. "Don't you see that whatever enters the mouth goes into the stomach and then out of the body? But the things that come out of the mouth come from the heart. And it is these things which make a person unclean. For out of the heart come evil thoughts, murder, adultery, sexual immorality, theft, false testimony, slander. These are what make a person unclean, but eating with unwashed hands does not make him unclean."

Jesus looked about at his men, then at Magdalene and Geshem, testing the understanding of each of them.

Magdalene felt that she understood his meaning. But she wondered if he understood how angry he had made the visiting Pharisees. He had sorely offended them. Of that she was certain. A fresh chill of fear curled through her, and in her spirit she sensed the beginning of a forewarning—a premonition of something unspeakable.

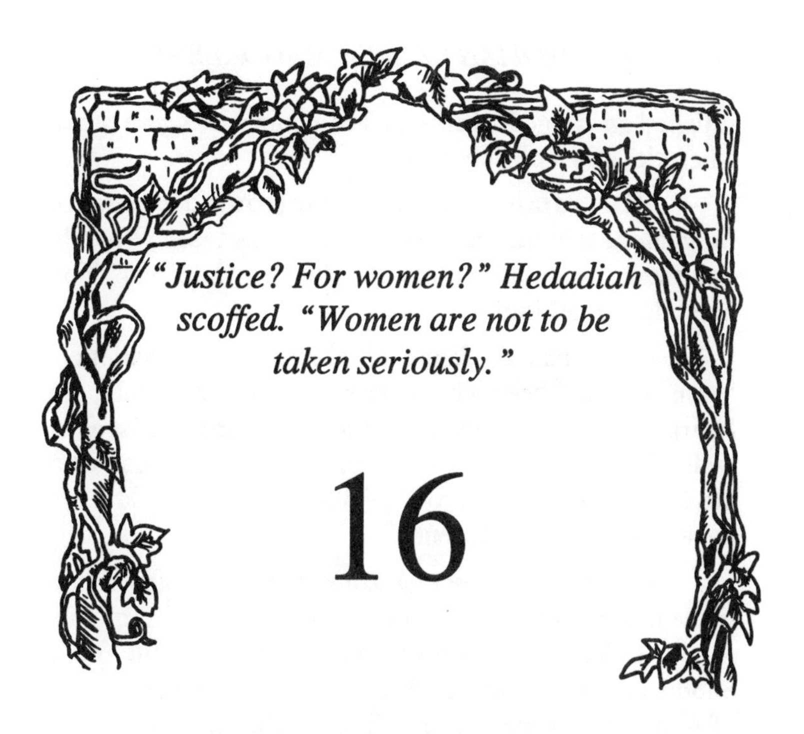

"Justice? For women?" Hedadiah scoffed. "Women are not to be taken seriously."

16

HAD MAGDALENE BEEN ABLE to travel back to Jerusalem with the visiting Pharisees, she would have realized that there was substance to the premonition forming in her spirit.

Her assessment of the visitors' resentment toward Jesus was accurate, for as soon as they arrived back in Jerusalem they wasted no time in going to the Chamber of Hewn Stone and reporting to Caiaphas and the Sanhedrin what Jesus had said.

The high priest's thin face darkened at the news. He turned to the elders assembled in the chamber and asked if there were others who knew of such blasphemy from the Nazarene.

A score of men rose to their feet. One by one, Caiaphas asked them to speak, and by the time they finished an image had emerged of a man who was a rebel, a heretic, and a blasphemer.

Hedadiah, who had confronted Jesus in Magdalene's home, now jumped from his seat. "What do you intend to do about this blasphemer, Caiaphas? You must do something!"

Caiaphas stiffened at Hedadiah's impatience. "You, and the three who were with you in Magdala, are Pharisees. And all who have spoken here are Pharisees as well. You know our rules. We must hear from those who are Sadducees. What proof of blasphemy do Sadducees have against this Nazarene?"

For a long moment, no one spoke. The only sound in the Chamber of Hewn Stone was the rustle of garments as the elders began turning and looking about for a Sadducee who would speak against Jesus. At last, Joseph of Arimathea, a merchant well-known for his good judgment and fair trade practices, rose slowly to his feet. He was a distinguished-looking man of medium height and portly figure. His eyes were the color of fine, aged amber, deep-set beneath bushy white eyebrows that matched his neatly trimmed beard.

The rustling sound stopped as those assembled settled back with respect to hear what he had to say.

"I believe as Sadducees do," Joseph began. "And yet I have no proof of blasphemy against the Nazarene. Rather, I have heard him say that he comes not to defy the Law but to fulfill it."

Hedadiah and the others shouted a cacophony of protest. Caiaphas pounded his staff of office against the stone floor to order them quiet. When at last they settled down, he nodded for Joseph to continue.

"I personally, and many of the people with whom I trade in Galilee and Decapolis, in Tyre and Sidon, and even here in Judea, have heard the teachings of this young rabbi. At no time have I heard him preach treason. At no time have I heard of him teaching heresy."

"What have you heard him preach?" Hedadiah challenged.

Joseph turned to him. "I have heard him honor the laws of Moses. I have seen his tenderness with children, and his justice for women."

"Justice? For women?" Hedadiah scoffed. Other Pharisees joined in:

"Women are not to be taken seriously."

"We don't even behold them with our eyes in public!"

"They are chattel."

"Women are here to do our bidding."

"What need for justice does a woman have?"

Again Caiaphas rapped his staff against the floor to regain order in the chamber. The question of justice for women meant little. The blasphemy of a heretic Galilean preacher probably meant even less. But Caiaphas's own personal authority as high priest was being challenged by Hedadiah and the others. He disliked that intensely. His control of the Sanhedrin meant everything.

Joseph waited patiently, eyeing the protestors. He noted that nearly all of them were Pharisees, men who followed the letter of the law with such fanaticism that its spirit was ignored. When order was once again restored, he turned to Caiaphas. "Honored priest, you asked for a Sadducee who had proof of blasphemy against Jesus of

Nazareth. I know of none. I only know that the Nazarene is a healer. He has healed all kinds of people of all kinds of diseases. He has even healed the child of one of Herod's own noblemen! There is no blasphemy in that. There is only blessing."

One of the other men with Hedadiah stood up. "Healing is not what we're talking about. He called us hypocrites!"

"But even worse," Hedadiah interrupted, "he spoke of himself as if he were God!"

Startled murmurs swept through the chamber and grew to a belligerent protest. This time Caiaphas did not rap for order. Instead, he sat stiffly in his chair, watching the protest and calculating what his next move should be.

Apparently no such calculation was needed by Joseph of Arimathea, who turned, walked out of the chamber, and headed toward the palace of Herod Antipas.

The sentries at the gate saluted smartly as Joseph approached, and a palace guard came quickly to escort him into the palace itself.

"I have come to see the honorable Chuza," Joseph told the guard as they entered a small vestibule.

The man nodded. "He is here today. I shall go and find him for you, sir, if you will wait here."

Joseph seated himself on a stone bench and thought again about the accusations Hedadiah and his companions had made against Jesus. All could be explained, and defended, except the last one. Had Hedadiah misunderstood, or had Jesus really told them that he was God?

The sound of footsteps distracted him. He glanced down the long corridor and saw Chuza coming toward him. As he stood, Chuza waved and hurried faster. "Joseph, my friend. Greetings of the day. How may I serve you?"

Joseph looked down the corridor to make certain no one else was within earshot, then spoke in a low tone. "I bring news of the Nazarene."

The smile on Chuza's round face disappeared. He, too, glanced about to make sure they were not being overheard.

"Where can we talk safely?" Joseph asked.

"In my private chambers. Joanna will want to hear this, too, and she is there." He turned and led the way down another long corridor to his private apartment. Once inside, he dismissed a servant, closed the door firmly and called to Joanna.

"My news concerns our friend the Nazarene," Joseph began when Joanna had joined them. He told them of the incident in the Chamber of Hewn Stone. "Hedadiah and his companions even report that Jesus spoke as if he were God Himself. Have you ever heard him say such a thing, Joanna?"

"I have," she nodded. "He has told many of us that he and his Father are one."

"And he does not mean his earthly father, the carpenter Joseph?" asked the merchant.

"No. I think he means that he and God are Father and son. That he and God are one."

"That is heresy for you Jews, isn't it?" Chuza asked.

"It is worse. It is blasphemy. And that is what they accuse him of."

Disturbed at the news, Joanna stood and walked away a few steps, deep in thought. Chuza explained. "Joanna believes he might be more than mere man." A frown of concern deepened on his face.

The merchant turned to her. "You must have good reason to believe such a thing."

"I do," she said. "I have been in his presence. I was with Magdalene when Jesus healed her. Together, we have traveled with him and his men in support of his ministry. He is more than mere man. There is a holiness about him, a power, that is hard to describe. But it is very real."

Chuza and Joseph looked at each other in silence, each considering Joanna's words and testing his own sense of belief against his knowledge of her sincerity and judgment.

She went back to stand near Chuza's chair. "When Magdalene first told me whom we were going in search of for her healing, it took all my strength not to chide or act in disbelief. And then, from the moment I saw Jesus, even before he had healed Magdalene, even before he had said a word to either of us, I knew that Magdalene had been right to search for him."

"But how did you know?" Joseph asked. "What did he do to make you feel that way?"

"Nothing. He was simply there."

Joseph frowned.

"There was about him an air of authority, a sense of power, supernatural power, that overwhelmed my spirit. In my heart, I knew this was a holy man. And now—if Jesus of Nazareth claims to be the Son of God as well as the Son of Man, I, for one, believe him."

Joseph gave a heavy sigh and leaned back in the chair.

"You don't believe me, do you?"

"Oh, I believe you," he said. "It is that no Pharisee will believe you. What you have told me is no proof of the Nazarene's divinity."

"Did Hedadiah report anything about this new kingdom which Jesus sometimes speaks of?" Chuza asked.

Joseph shook his head. "He only reported that Jesus claimed to be God. And that he had called Hedadiah and the others hypocrites!"

Joanna smiled in spite of the seriousness of the situation.

"What action will they now take?" Chuza asked.

"They will want to exile him. Or imprison him. Or—"

"Or what?" Joanna insisted.

"Or kill him."

Joanna gasped at the thought. Chuza reached for her hand and protectively clasped it in his own. Their guest stood, wandered toward the window and stared moodily out onto the palace gardens. The flowering shrubs were in their last flambuoyant issue of color before harvest time. Within another few days, the Feast of Tabernacles would be in full celebration of the blessings of harvest. Jerusalem would fill with celebrants from all over Judea, Galilee, the Decapolis and lands beyond. All good

Jews would try to come. Only Passover in the spring would attract more pilgrims.

"Will Jesus be coming to Jerusalem for the Feast of Tabernacles?"

"I—I don't know," Joanna replied.

"Can you get a message of warning to him?"

Joanna looked at Chuza. "Could we send Razis?"

Her husband thought for a moment.

"We could at least send the message to Magdalene, couldn't we?" Joanna urged. "She would see that it got to Jesus."

"Very well," Chuza agreed, getting to his feet. "Prepare the message, my wife. Send Razis to Magdalene."

"And I, in the meantime," said Joseph, "will do what I can to discredit Hedadiah's report among my brethren in the Sanhedrin."

"And I will alert Herod to expect another visit from Caiaphas," Chuza offered. "Since there was no mention of a new kingdom for the high priest to report, I expect that Herod will have little time for any other complaints."

"Thank you for coming, Joseph," Joanna said. "Your friendship is always comforting."

He smiled, bowed, and followed Chuza out of the apartment.

By the time the message of warning reached Magdala, Jesus had already told his men that he wanted them to go to the Feast of Tabernacles without him.

Some of them who were with him in the back courtyard of Geshem's house argued with him about it.

From the weaving room, Magdalene overheard the argument. She stopped her work and went to the door where she could hear them better. Hannah, who had been working alongside her, did likewise.

"You ought to leave here," said Matthew. "Go to Judea so that your followers there may see the miracles you do."

"And you should take Magdalene with you," John urged. "Let her witness there about her healing, as she has witnessed elsewhere."

"Since you are doing these things, show yourself to the world," Peter agreed.

"No one who wants to become a public figure acts in secret," James urged.

Jesus listened patiently to his men, then replied softly. "The right time for me has not yet come."

"Maybe it is not the right time for us, then," Thomas suggested from the other side of the courtyard.

"For you, any time is right," Jesus said. "The world does not yet hate you. But the world hates me."

A shiver went through Magdalene as he said these words. Hannah noticed and put her arm around her.

"Why should the world hate you, Lord?" Judas asked.

Jesus turned a level gaze on him. "The world hates me because I testify that what it does is evil."

Judas looked away, as if uncomfortable under Jesus' steady gaze.

Concern filled the faces of the others.

"You go to the feast," Jesus said. "I am not going up to this feast because for me the right time has not yet come." He stood, left the courtyard and headed toward the lakeshore.

"Go with him, my daughter," Hannah urged Magdalene. "He is too much alone in recent days. He needs a friend. His destiny weighs heavily on him, I think."

Magdalene caught up with Jesus as he neared the water's edge. "I should like to be with you for a while, my friend," she said gently.

He smiled at her, but said nothing. He reached down, picked up a pebble and cast it far out into the water, and watched the ripples spread in ever-widening circles.

She expected him to say a parable. Certainly the ever-widening ripples made her think of how his actions affected people far removed from the center of his being. But he said not a word.

Instead, he turned and began to walk slowly along the shore, looking back to see if she was following and, with another smile, encouraging her to do so.

She caught up to him, then kept pace with his long stride as best she could. Deep inside, her heart was singing with joy. How she loved him. How safe and how right she felt whenever she was with him. The only thing that could make their moments of companionship more complete for her would be if they could marry.

But that was an impossibility that she long since had realized. Her love for him had to be of a different kind, just as his love for her was different. He was God's man. Not hers. He might even be God Himself.

She cast a quick glance at him. His face was somber. There was no fear, but the seriousness of a destiny recognized was clearly evident. The joy in her heart abated, replaced by a sense of worry that the world hated him. If they knew him as she did, how could they hate him?

He knew her thoughts. "After my brothers leave for the Feast of Tabernacles," he said, "I am going in secret to Jerusalem myself. It is important that I do so."

"I want to go with you," she said without hesitation.

"I must go into the Temple courts and teach."

"I have much to learn."

A look of gentle love washed over his face.

"Joanna knows believers who need a testimony like mine. She will provide housing and food for me," Magdalene urged, and then as if in afterthought, she said, "and for you, too, if you don't mind staying in the house of Herod Antipas."

Jesus glanced at her, startled, then exploded in laughter. "Ah, the irony of it," he said. He reached for her hand, squeezed it, and brought it to his lips. "Thank you, my friend. You are dear to me beyond your imaginings."

"Go and arrest him, Roman,"
the man in the blue robes
urged Domenicus.
17

AT TIMES OF FESTIVALS, Jerusalem was a city bloated with strangers. Her streets were more crowded than ever. Pilgrims' tents covered the hills outside the city walls. And for this particular festival, the Feast of Tabernacles, booths and shelters of every kind and description cluttered the city inside and out. Domenicus didn't like it.

In fact, he didn't like any of the Jewish festivals. They intruded on the normal routine of things, forcing assignment of additional soldier patrols. He even had been assigned command of a street patrol near the Temple Mount. He especially didn't like that.

He was no soldier—not for this kind of occasion, he told himself, observing the mass of humanity in the Porches of Solomon and the Gentiles Court. The festival was half over and still there were thousands of pilgrims here. If a disturbance arose, it would be more than his squad of twenty soldiers could handle.

He motioned for the squad to pair off and expand their patrol of the area. As for himself, he turned toward the shade of the Porches of Solomon and began to slowly walk their length. Pilgrims, both men and women, stood about in small groups quietly talking among themselves. Others were seated on the long stone benches built against the outer walls. All seemed peaceful enough, he supposed, even though a very large crowd was a short distance ahead of him on the western end of the portico.

At least he hoped they would be peaceful. The crowd was too large for one man to control. He hesitated and glanced about for his soldiers in case he should need them, but none of them were in sight. Cautiously, hand on the hilt of his dagger, he once more moved forward until he was at the edge of the throng. There he could hear the voice of the person addressing the crowd, but he couldn't see him.

He strained to stand taller and peer across the shoulders of people in front of him. To no avail. The teacher apparently was seated on one of the stone benches. Domenicus turned to the man next to him. "Who is speaking?"

"The Nazarene."

Domenicus stiffened with surprise. "The Nazarene? You mean Jesus of Nazareth?"

The man nodded. "And isn't it amazing?"

"What?"

"That he should be able to teach in this way?"

Domenicus made a scoffing sound. "What is more amazing is that he should be allowed to teach! He is a heretic."

Several men who were nearby turned to look at him. Seeing that he was in Roman uniform, most dismissed his comment and turned their attention back to Jesus.

From the other side of the crowd, a man called out to Jesus. "How did you get such learning without having studied?"

Jesus answered, "My teaching is not my own. It comes from Him who sent me. If anyone chooses to do God's will, he will find out whether my teaching comes from God or whether I speak on my own."

"Heresy!" someone shouted.

Jesus ignored the shout. "He who speaks on his own does so to bring honor to himself. There is nothing false about him."

A man dressed in blue robes joined the crowd and stood directly behind Domenicus. "Isn't this the man they are trying to kill?" he asked.

"He is the man," Domenicus said, without glancing around. "It will be good riddance."

"But how can he be here speaking publicly? Have the authorities really concluded that he is the Christ?"

"How could a Roman know that?" Domenicus said sharply. He gestured to the man standing next to him. "Ask this Jew about such things."

"I doubt that the Nazarene is the Christ," the Jew said. "We know where he comes from. When the Christ comes, no one will know where he comes from."

As if he had overheard their conversation, Jesus suddenly cried out, "Yes, you know me. And you know where I am from. I am not here on my own, but He who sent me is true. You do not know Him. But I know Him because I am from Him and He sent me."

"Go and arrest him, Roman," the man in the blue robes urged Domenicus.

"That's the duty of the Temple guards," Domenicus said.

"I see no Temple guards here," retorted the man, pushing at him. "Go forward! Arrest him!"

The buffeting stirred Domenicus's anger. He pulled his dagger and whirled about, only to find himself face-to-face with Caiaphas, the high priest.

Caiaphas also was surprised. The priest's face went pale as he stepped back, giving himself wide distance from the dagger. Others who had been standing close moved away, making room for a fight.

"A thousand pardons, sir," Domenicus hurriedly apologized, and shoved the dagger back into its holster.

Caiaphas studied him through narrowed eyes.

"I meant no harm to your honorable person," Domenicus explained. "I simply was reacting to someone pushing me."

"I should have pushed you sooner," came Caiaphas's angry reply. "His men are now alerted. You have lost your chance to arrest him!"

"I was not sent here to arrest anyone."

"Your Tribune Fortunatas shall hear of your failure. And of your assault upon me."

Before Domenicus could utter another word of defense or explanation, Caiaphas strode off in the direction of the Chamber of Hewn Stone.

"He will return with the Temple guards, I expect," said the Jew standing next to Domenicus.

Some of the crowd drifted away, not wanting to be involved if Caiaphas did come back with the Temple guards. Some stayed, among them many Pharisees. Others stayed, too, still listening to Jesus and asking among themselves, "When the Christ comes, will he do more miraculous signs than this man?"

Domenicus glanced toward Jesus who was still sitting on the stone bench, seemingly unmoved by the disturbance or by fear. "I am with you for only a short time," Jesus said. "And then I go to the one who sent me. You will look for me but you will not find me; and where I am, you cannot come."

The Jews standing beside Domenicus said to one another, "What does he mean by that?"

"Where could he go that we could not find him?"

"Will he go where our people live scattered among the Greeks, and teach the Greeks?"

They had only questions, no answers.

At that moment, Caiaphas and the chief priests returned with the Temple guards. They pushed and shoved at the crowd to get to Jesus, but the crowd gave way slowly, and when the group finally reached the front of the throng, one of the priests cursed.

Jesus had disappeared.

"His time has not yet come," a man near

Domenicus said softly. "They will arrest him only when he is ready."

The Temple guards turned on the crowd, dispersing it, before following Caiaphas and the other priests away from the portico.

Within just a few moments, Domenicus discovered that he was alone except for two women and their manservant standing near the stone bench where Jesus had been sitting. They were watching him. And despite the distance that separated him from them, he thought there was something familiar about them.

The taller of the two women waved and started walking toward him. He took a step or two in her direction and then recognized who it was. It was his sister Magdalene! He stopped short. Why was she here in Jerusalem? And why was she here on the Temple Mount with the heretic Jesus? Before the questions fully formed in his mind, he knew the answers to them. Jesus was why she was in Jerusalem. Jesus was why she was on the Temple Mount.

Abruptly, he realized something else. His sister most probably was among those who traveled with Jesus to witness for him! He cursed and turned away, regretting that he had not done what Caiaphas had tried to push him to do. He should have arrested Jesus. Authorized or not, he should have done it. If given another chance, he would not fail.

He reached the edge of the portico, hurried across the open expanse of the Gentiles Court, and took the steps two at a time down from the Temple Mount. By the time he reached the Viaduct which led into the Upper City, he realized that the woman with Magdalene was Joanna. She was a Jesus-believer, too, no doubt. That would explain why Chuza had been so aloof when Domenicus had gone to the palace to pay his respects to Joanna. The realization caused him to pause midway across the Viaduct and consider how he might use such knowledge in his own behalf, as well as to be rid of Jesus.

"If he returns," Joanna's note concluded, "he will be captured and killed. It has all been planned."

18

THE BEGINNING OF THE END was near. In her heart, Magdalene knew it.

During the six months which followed the disturbance on the Temple Mount, many signs pointed to the unthinkable fact that one day soon the foes of Jesus would prevail.

The first sign, of course, had been the words Jesus used in response to the Pharisees that day on the Temple Mount. "You will look for me," he had said. "But you will not find me; and where I am, you cannot come."

She still wondered if he meant those words just for the Pharisees, or if he had also meant them for those who were believers. She found them troublesome because she had the feeling that she was as close to him as she ever would be, or ever could be. And it occurred to her more and more often that many of his words remained cloaked in a mystery beyond her understanding.

Increasingly, those who opposed him gained in numbers. Fear seemed to take over the hearts of many who had followed him, and they no longer wanted to be seen in his company.

It made no difference to Jesus. He continued to teach and preach throughout Judea and Perea. And he continued to heal. In Jerusalem, just before she had returned to Magdala to help her parents fill a large weaving order, she had watched him heal a crippled woman and a man who had been born blind. But because Jesus had healed the crippled woman on a Sabbath, he had incurred additional wrath from those who opposed him. With the resurrection of his friend Lazarus in Bethany of Judea, the pressures for his arrest intensified to such a feverish pitch that Jesus and the twelve returned to Galilee.

At the close of the month which the Romans called February, the Sanhedrin issued warrants for his arrest. Notices were posted in the major towns of Judea. In other towns, a court crier publicly announced the notice.

Joanna sent news of the warrant to Magdalene by Razis, and in the same message urged her to warn Jesus to never again return to Judea. *If he returns,* Joanna's note concluded, *he will be captured and killed. It all has been carefully planned.* Enclosed with her message was a copy of the original handbill.

Magdalene read it, her heart breaking as she grimly passed it to Geshem to read aloud for the benefit of Hannah and Razis. Tobias had appeared in the doorway behind her. With him were other household servants. Geshem motioned for them to enter the room to hear the dreadful news, and then began to read from the official handbill:

> Wanted for Arrest: Yeshu Hannosri or Jesus the Nazarene.
>
> He shall be stoned because he has practiced sorcery and enticed Israel to apostasy. Anyone who can say anything in his favor, let him come forward and plead on his behalf. Anyone who knows where he is, let him declare it to the Great Sanhedrin in Jerusalem.

A soft moaning sound came from the servants.

Tobias and Razis bowed their heads dejectedly.

As Geshem crumpled the parchment, Magdalene hid her face in her hands. Hannah came to her, embraced her, and began to sob.

"Jesus must be warned," Geshem said.

Magdalene straightened. "You are right, my father. We must not assume that he already knows about this."

"I will carry the message," Razis offered, "if you will tell me where to find him."

Magdalene shook her head. "Thank you, Razis, but I must carry the message to him." She slipped free of Hannah's embrace, went to Geshem and pulled the parchment from his clenched hand.

"Tobias should go with you, my daughter," he said.

She agreed and, within a short time, they set out. By the time they reached Capernaum and inquired at the house of Zebedee for Jesus, twilight had settled across the land and an early moon was rising.

"Jesus is down by the lake with James and John," Salome told her, and pointed toward a nearby area of the shoreline where part of Zebedee's fishing fleet was at rest. "Do you want me to go with you? I'll be glad to."

Magdalene declined with thanks, then turned and walked in the direction Salome had pointed. Tobias kept close to her. They crested a rise of land that separated the house from the lake. A small campfire flickered near one of the fishing boats. Jesus, James and John hunkered near it, talking. As Magdalene and Tobias came within view of the firelight, Jesus noticed them and came toward them.

A mixture of joy and sorrow flooded through Magdalene at the sight of him. He seemed taller than ever, stronger than ever, his physique backlighted as it was by the flickering campfire. How could this man who had done so much good for so many people now be the victim of jealousy and greed and fear from those in authority in Jerusalem? She forced herself not to run to him and embrace him in a display of unseemly emotion.

"Magdalene, my friend," he said, stopping in front of her and looking at her in his familiar, penetrating way. "You are troubled. How can I help you?"

The emotion of what she knew was overwhelming now. She sank to her knees and blurted, "Oh dear Jesus, they want to arrest you. The warrant has been written. They will kill you."

His expression did not change.

James and John had risen to their feet. As if sensing the need to leave Jesus and Magdalene alone, they motioned for Tobias to join them as they headed back toward the house. When the three had disappeared behind the rise, Jesus reached down, lifted Magdalene to her feet and wrapped his arms about her in a comforting embrace. "I thank you for your concern, and for your warning. But there is something that you, above all others, must understand. The hour soon will come for the Son of Man to be glorified."

"Where is the glory in death?" she resisted, pressing her head closer to his chest. To her, the deep, rhythmic pumping of his heart seemed eternal. She embraced him as if her own arms could protect him from death.

"Do not be sad for me, Magdalene," he said. "I go to fulfill my destiny."

No longer could she hold back her tears. They poured forth from a well of such deep sorrow that her whole body trembled as it had not done since before she was healed of her dreadful affliction.

For a time, Jesus said nothing more. He simply held her until her sobbing abated. Then he tucked one hand under her chin, tilted her head back and once again looked deep into her eyes.

She pulled a square of cotton from her cloak. Jesus took it and wiped the tears from her face. "My heart is troubled too," he said. "But what shall I say?"

"There must be something we can do."

He released her from his embrace and they began to walk along the shoreline. "Peter said a similar thing to me, Magdalene."

"What did you tell Peter?"

"I told him he should not put temptation before me."

She glanced sharply at him. "Temptation?"

He nodded. "Fulfillment of destiny is not always easy. And in my case, what am I to do? What shall I say? 'Father, save me from this hour?'"

She stopped, turned and searched his face. Moonlight was fully upon it, revealing an odd mixture of human agony and sublime resolve. For the first time, she began to realize that the Son of Man must indeed be who he claimed to be: the Son of God.

"How can I ask my Father to save me," Jesus asked rhetorically, "when it is for this very reason that He sent me and that my time now approaches?"

Magdalene glanced away and stared out across the waters of the lake, following the trail of moonlight with her eyes while her mind searched for a reasonable answer other than the one he gave. But there was no other answer. She knew it in her spirit.

Jesus took her by the arm and began to walk once more. "I shall go to Jerusalem for Passover. There, the words of the prophets, and my purpose, will be fulfilled."

"I shall go with you," she said without hesitation.

He smiled at her. "You are my constant and true friend. Since boyhood, I have loved you."

"Say nothing more until we are in my own chambers. Spies are everywhere."

19

MAGDALENE INTERPRETED Jesus' words as approving of her going to Jerusalem with him and his men. But the next morning she discovered that she was wrong. They had left quite early.

"They left before daylight," Zebedee said when she and Susanna, with whom she and Tobias had stayed, got to his house.

"Before daylight? But I expected to travel with them. And Susanna was going, too."

Zebedee shrugged. "All I know is that my entire household has gone off with him! Salome, James and John, even some of the fishermen who work for me. All of them. Off to Passover in Jerusalem." He shrugged again and started to go back into the house, but then stopped short and looked at Magdalene. "Oh yes! There is one other thing. Jesus said he wanted you to return to Magdala—to safety."

Susanna turned to Magdalene, her eyes large with surprise and uncertainty. "What a peculiar message. Why should Jesus think there would be danger for you in Jerusalem?"

Magdalene did not answer, remembering the gravity of the conversation she had had with Jesus the evening before. Perhaps her safety had been Jesus' reason for leaving without her.

"Well, what do we do now?" Susanna asked. "Shall I return to Magdala with you? Or stay here?"

"You are always welcome at my house. You know that."

They bid farewell to Zebedee and began the journey back to Magdala. As always, her parents welcomed Susanna as their guest. But they appeared disturbed when Magdalene told them of her conversation with Jesus and all that had happened. "So I have returned here as he bade me to do," she concluded. "Apparently I cannot help him."

"Nonsense!" Hannah answered to her daughter's surprise. "Your friend Jesus is in trouble. You still must go to Jerusalem and try to help him."

"Your mother is right, Magdalene," Geshem agreed. "You must seek help for him. Through Joanna's husband Chuza. Surely with his powerful position in Herod's court, he can do something."

Her parents' sense of urgency about helping Jesus surprised and pleased her. In the months of being away and traveling with him, she had begun to think of herself only as Jesus' helper. Now she was reminded that her parents, too, counted Jesus as their friend. They had liked him as a boy. And in his manhood they, too, loved and supported him.

"And if, for some reason, Joanna's husband cannot help," Hannah said, "you can always ask for help from Tribune Fortunatas. I heard him tell you that."

Of course! Fortunatas! How foolish of her not to think of him before. She turned to Susanna. "Do you still want to go to Jerusalem for your people's Passover celebration?"

Susanna nodded. "But I much more want to go to help our friend Jesus."

"I will send a servant to tell Joanna you will be coming," Geshem said.

The following morning, Magdalene, Susanna and Tobias began the journey to Jerusalem. Geshem had suggested they go the shorter route through Samaria. "The Samaritans have no quarrel with Greeks. And Susanna will be safe with you and Tobias," he said. "Make stops at Sychar and Ephraim. Stay with people we do business with, Magdalene."

Geshem paused, then gave another reason for taking the Samaritan route. "If I know Jesus like I think I do, he will not go straight to Jerusalem. His good friend Lazarus lives in Bethany, and I'm sure Jesus will want to stay with him a few days. You might even be able to arrive in Jerusalem before he does."

This they did, and on the afternoon of the third day they arrived on Jerusalem's outskirts. The roads leading into the city were alive with pilgrims. The hills were like a fine harvest of color with the scattering of their tents. Magdalene was amazed, for as large as the crowds had been which had followed Jesus, they could not compare with the number of people she now saw.

"Passover is the most important of all our feasts," Susanna said respectfully, her eyes also wide with wonder at the sight of the crowds.

"Come, Mistress Magdalene," said Tobias. "It will take some time to get through these crowds. And the Lady Joanna will be expecting us before darkness falls."

Magdalene did not argue. She was more anxious than any of them to reach Joanna and her husband, to talk with Chuza about helping Jesus. She took Susanna's hand so they would not get separated, and followed Tobias down the hill into the slow-moving crowd and eventually passed through the Damascus Road Gate into the city itself.

Once inside the city walls, Tobias led them to a less-crowded side street. Here they were able to move more quickly toward the Viaduct and into the Upper City. Within another few minutes, they passed through the gates of Herod's palace.

Joanna was waiting for them in the palace gardens. She nodded to Tobias, greeted Magdalene and Susanna with hugs and whispered, "Say nothing until we are in my own chambers. Spies are everywhere." She turned and led the way across the gardens into a small door almost hidden by a large acacia tree.

Inside, a poorly-lit passage led to another door which opened into the wide bright room that Magdalene remembered from her earlier visits.

Joanna carefully locked the door behind them as her servant, Eglah, came and took their cloaks. To Tobias, Joanna said, "You will stay here in our private apartment with Razis and Eglah. Do not go about the palace unless they are with you."

Tobias nodded, bowed and helped Eglah remove the luggage.

With a flush of excitement and nervousness, Joanna embraced Magdalene and Susanna once more. "Oh, I am glad to see you two. Your servant arrived yesterday with the message that you were coming." She hesitated, glanced about and said in a more hushed tone, "Were you able to warn Jesus?"

"Yes, I warned him," Magdalene told her. "But it did no good. He is on his way to Jerusalem."

A look of fear crossed Joanna's face.

"Cannot your husband do something to help him?"

Joanna shook her head.

"But may I speak with him about it?"

"Of course. Chuza always welcomes you, Magdalene. And he will listen to whatever you need to say to him. But—"

"But he will do nothing?"

"He cannot. The Sanhedrin's anger is like a pox. Chuza cannot stand against it. Not even Herod Antipas can stand against it. Even if he wanted to. Which he doesn't, of course."

"Is there no fairness in him at all?" Magdalene asked.

A smile of resignation crossed Joanna's face. "When it benefits him, yes." She moved away from them and strolled to the windows overlooking the palace gardens.

"Maybe you could speak again with Jesus, Magdalene," Susanna suggested.

Joanna questioned Magdalene with a look.

"His mind is set," Magdalene answered sadly. "Besides, my mother thinks I should speak with the Tribune Fortunatas about this. She thinks he might be able to help."

"Is that the man Domenicus works for?"

She nodded as Joanna's soft laugh of disapproval made clear the foolishness of her mother's suggestion. Her heart sank. She had been grasping at straws.

"But I thought Fortunatas felt differently about Jesus than Domenicus does," Susanna said.

"How do you know that?" asked Joanna.

"Magdalene told me."

Joanna turned her quizzical look toward Magdalene.

"Fortunatas came to see me before he moved to Jerusalem," Magdalene explained. "He was full of questions about my healing. He did not scoff at it, nor at Jesus. I thought him sincere. I have even held hopes that his good attitude would affect Domenicus and make him less hostile."

Joanna led them away from the windows to a grouping of chairs and motioned for them to be seated. "I'm afraid your hopes for Domenicus are ill-placed, Magdalene."

"Yes, I know. He totally ignored us both when we saw him on the Temple Mount."

"He has been even more hostile since then. He is now an active agitator against Jesus."

Magdalene felt a sudden rush of fear well up inside her. "In what way?"

"First, he attached himself to one of the high priest's aides and spread lies about Jesus being a charlatan and a sorcerer. Next, he tried to make friends with one of Chuza's aides and told him he knew that I was a Jesus-believer. He said he had proof of it, and that the aide could elevate his position if he would report such treason to Herod Antipas and have me banished."

Magdalene felt sick inside.

"Fortunately, the young aide is loyal to my husband. He reported the incident to him. In turn, Chuza posted notices that Domenicus was considered a threat to the court and was never to be admitted again to the palace."

Their conversation halted abruptly when Eglah brought refreshments for the women. Magdalene welcomed the interruption. She felt wounded by the litany of treachery which Joanna was reciting, and she needed a moment to sort it all out. It was one thing for Domenicus to be jealous of her as his sister, but to attack Joanna and to stir anger against Jesus was beyond anything she had ever thought him capable of doing. He would have to be stopped. Some way, somehow, Domenicus would have to be stopped.

Joanna watched Eglah leave before continuing her report on Domenicus. "The most recent thing we have heard is that Domenicus is in the pay of the Pharisees to bring them proof that Jesus is a blasphemer. It is also said that one of Jesus' own men is in the pay of the Pharisees. It will be his job to deliver Jesus into the hands of the Sanhedrin."

"No," Susanna gasped softly. Magdalene was also having trouble believing the news, but the ill feeling inside her told her it was true. One of the twelve . . .

Joanna went on. "You see, when Jesus raised Lazarus from the dead, the priesthood and the Sanhedrin feared for their lives. Here was a man who had powers that none of them could equal. Nor could they explain why he would do such a thing, or how he could have done it. They panicked. That's when they posted the arrest warrant which I sent to you. And now the city swarms with spies and soldiers in plain dress and Temple guards who have been promised bonuses for the capture of the Nazarene. He will be caught. He will be killed."

The silence which now enveloped them was somber and as dark as the cloak of a night without starlight. The heaviness of dread pressed against Magdalene, her mind reeling against disbelief. Outraged at the circumstance, bereaved by Domenicus's involvement, she fought for a single, small, hopeful thought. Something must be done.

She must do something. She pushed up out of her chair and paced to the window. Darkness was approaching the land. In the distance, she could hear the sounds of a city bloated with pilgrims who had come to pray and worship and celebrate. But there was no celebration in her heart. Nor in the hearts of those who were her friends. She must do something.

"Joanna," she turned. "I must see and talk with

Fortunatas. Will you allow Razis to escort me to the Roman headquarters?"

Before Joanna could answer, a door at the far end of the room opened admitting Chuza and Razis. Chuza waved a greeting and came toward them. "Ah, Magdalene. It is good to see you again. And Susanna." He bowed to them both, then went to Joanna and kissed her hand.

"I have told them the bad news about Domenicus," Joanna said.

A peculiar look crossed Chuza's face.

"What is it, my husband?" Joanna asked, alarmed.

He made a gesture in half-apology, half-regret. "I bring more bad news."

Magdalene felt a lump rise in her throat. "About Jesus?"

He nodded. "About Jesus. He is here. In Jerusalem. He's been here several days."

A new sense of hope and relief sprang up in Magdalene. "And he's still all right? They haven't arrested him and he's been here several days?"

Chuza widened his eyes, surprised at her optimism.

"Then maybe he is safe after all. Maybe he will not be arrested!" But even as she said it, Magdalene remembered what Jesus himself had told her only a few days before.

Chuza came to her. "I am told that Jesus rode into the city on a young donkey, and that the people in the streets were in a frenzy of delight at the sight of him. They laid palm fronds on the streets. They shouted *Hosannas* to him and hailed him as their king."

"When was this?" Magdalene asked.

"On the day after the Jews' Sabbath. Just a few days past."

"Why are you just now being told of this, my husband?" Joanna asked.

He turned. "You'll recall that you and I and most of the rest of the court were in a hunting party—up in the hills near Emmaus with the tetrarch and his lady!"

"Oh yes. How could I have forgotten . . . "

"Exactly! The memory of the hunting party was as unimportant to you, my wife, as Jesus' arrival in Jerusalem was to most people here in the palace." Chuza shrugged. "No one thought even to mention it until today when Caiaphas came to see Herod and told him about it, and urged him to arrest Jesus."

"Caiaphas?" Magdalene asked in surprise. "But I thought he wanted the Sanhedrin to arrest Jesus."

"Not if someone else will do it for him." Chuza rubbed his palms together and paced away thoughtfully. "Caiaphas is afraid of the crowds. Jesus is very popular with them, and that's why Caiaphas has not yet arrested him. He fears a public riot, and trouble with the Romans."

Magdalene straightened. "Then there is hope for Jesus' safety, after all."

Chuza turned to her and shook his head in a regretful manner. "It is only a matter of time."

"I understand there is nothing you can do to help him," Magdalene said. "But I was hoping to speak with the Roman Tribune Fortunatas, and seek his help."

Chuza's round face darkened with concern.

"Just before you came in, my husband, she was asking if you would let Razis escort her to Roman headquarters," Joanna added.

The frown deepened on Chuza's face.

"Magdalene thinks that the tribune might have some concern for Jesus that most Romans wouldn't have."

Chuza turned to Magdalene. "You have good evidence of that, do you?"

"I believe I do. From a conversation he and I had when he was a guest in my father's house."

Chuza stood quietly, considering the request. Through the window, Magdalene could see that darkness had blanketed the holy city. Here and there, torches flared and made orange patches against the darkness. The door at the far end of the room opened again, and Eglah entered with a lighted brand. Razis took it from her and went about the room lighting torches and setting them in wall braziers.

Chuza spoke. "I think it would be a waste of your time. But if you wish to see Fortunatas, I will permit Razis to escort you. But you must take your man Tobias with you too."

The next morning, at a time which Chuza had told her would be appropriate for such a visit, Magdalene and Tobias followed Razis through the wide street leading from Herod's palace to the Hasmonean Palace which the Romans used as their headquarters. To Magdalene's surprise, she saw no sentries at the entrance.

"It is because of the crowds of pilgrims in the city," Razis explained. "Every available man is on patrol in the streets."

Inside, they found themselves in a great reception hall, and asked an officer where they might find the Tribune Fortunatas. He pointed to an alcove off the main hall. They went toward it and pushed aside a woven drapery that separated the alcove from the main passageway. Fortunatas stood frowning over a large table on which was a map of the city.

"Good morning, sir," Magdalene said, stopping just inside the drapery. "It is Magdalene, from the house of Geshem in Magdala."

The frown changed abruptly to a surprised smile. Fortunatas came around the table toward her, his hands extended in welcome. "How good it is to see you again, my lady. How very good, indeed."

"You remember Tobias," Magdalene said by way of introduction. "And this is Razis of the house of Chuza."

Fortunatas looked startled. "You mean Chuza of the palace of Herod?"

All three of them nodded.

"Then you have come on serious business."

"I have," Magdalene said. "And it may well be confidential business."

"Confidential? Then it is about Domenicus?"

"No, it is not about Domenicus."

"It is just as well. I have had to let him go. His services are no longer useful."

Magdalene glanced at Tobias and saw in his eyes

the same question that was in her mind. What would happen to Domenicus now?

Fortunatas lowered his voice, "If you have not come about your brother, then you must have come about your friend Jesus."

She nodded.

He turned and led them all to a grouping of chairs away from the drapery through which they had come, and motioned for them to be seated. He sat down facing them. "I doubt that I can help you. This is a fight between the Jews themselves, their priesthood, their Sanhedrin. They are trying to involve Herod Antipas, and that sly fox, as your Jesus calls him, is trying to involve Pilate."

"Then there is nothing that can be done to keep him from being arrested?" Magdalene asked the question resignedly, realizing it was a useless one, knowing only that she had to be in Jerusalem to help him if she could.

Fortunatas reached out and took her hand. "There are only two things you can do for Jesus now, Magdalene."

"And what are they?"

"Let him know you're in Jerusalem because you are still his friend. And when it all happens, care for his body."

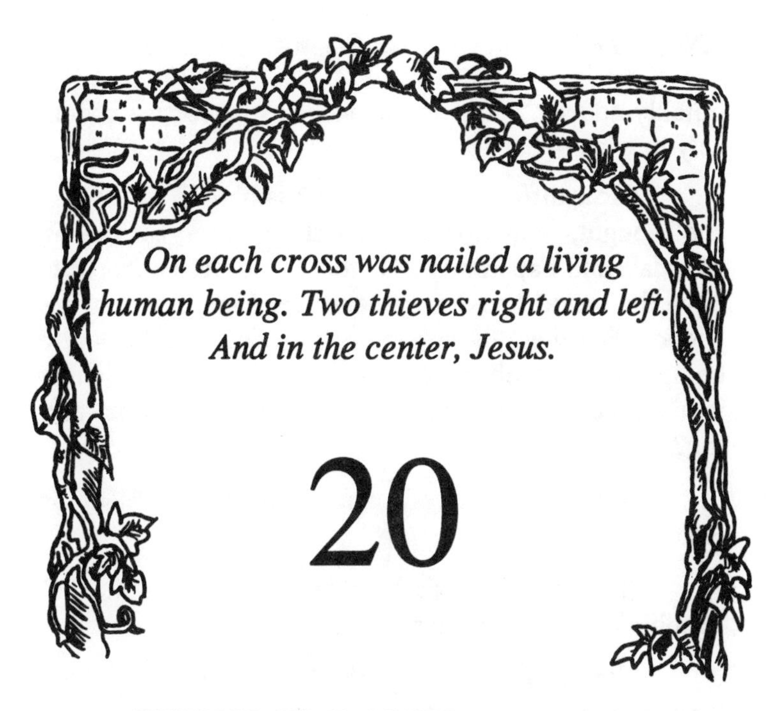

On each cross was nailed a living human being. Two thieves right and left. And in the center, Jesus.
20

WHEN IT ALL HAPPENS . . .

She let the repetition of his words trail into sorrowful silence. Heaviness dragged at her heart, pulled at her hopes.

"Where is Jesus staying?" Tobias asked.

"I don't know," Fortunatas said. "He comes and goes. From the house of Lazarus in Bethany to the homes of various friends here in Jerusalem. One of them is said to be here in the Upper City."

"Do you know the name of his friend?" Magdalene asked.

Fortunatas shook his head and said gently, "His friends in Jerusalem are careful to guard their own identities." He saw the startled look on Magdalene's face and quickly added, "They do this to be as protective of him as you wish to be."

How different it was for Jesus here in Jerusalem, she thought, remembering how it had been for him in Magdala and Capernaum. There, people were honored to have the world know they cared for him and were his friends. But then, there had been no danger attached to being his friend. She rose to her feet. "How much danger is involved in trying to find the house where he is staying?"

An expression of pained surprise crossed the Roman's face.

Tobias and Razis both protested. "Too much!" "Unthinkable, my mistress."

Sincerity was plain in their faces. Reason told her they were right. But her hurt and anger at the circumstances threatening Jesus made her bold, made her consider what was beyond reason.

"I pray that you are not seriously considering such a thing," Fortunatas added, coming to her. "Tobias and Razis are right. There is great danger. You must not do it."

"But you said I should let him know that I am here in Jerusalem," she reminded him.

"That does not mean you should go looking for him yourself, Magdalene."

Tobias also came to her. "My mistress, think of how the Lord has tried to keep you from danger. He would not let you go with him from Capernaum. He knew the dangers then. He knows them now. It is a grievous time for him. Why add to his burden by placing yourself in danger?"

From beyond the quietness of Fortunatas's room, Magdalene heard the heavy tramp of soldiers' feet and the muted sounds of commands being given. They reinforced the truth of Tobias's words. For the first time, she acknowledged that there was a limit to how much she could share in Jesus' tribulations. Slowly, she nodded and turned away.

Fortunatas followed her. "Promise me you will not attempt to seek out his other friends here in Jerusalem."

She looked at him but said nothing.

"Promise me that," he insisted. "And I will see that Jesus learns of your presence here in the city, and that you are safe."

"Very well," she agreed, her resistance defeated and her shoulders sagging. "I promise you that."

She was true to her word. For the rest of that day and during all of the next, she stayed close by the private apartments of Joanna and Chuza in the palace of Herod Antipas. But her heart was heavy and she felt uneasy.

Susanna went to the house of a Jewish friend to observe Passover. Tobias made himself useful by helping Razis and Eglah with their chores. Magdalene felt useless. Her mind was constantly on Jesus and her heart continually in prayer for him. Time passed slowly.

There was no word from Fortunatas. Her restlessness disturbed Joanna, who finally insisted that they go into the Upper Agora, the great open market filled with the luxuries and treasures of many lands.

Magdalene found the noise and the crowds in the marketplace unsettling and irritating. At one point, she thought she saw Peter and John haggling with a wine merchant. But before she could be certain, they were lost to her view. It only added to her frustration. Joanna, too, found no joy in shopping, and soon suggested they return to the palace for a walk in its beautiful gardens.

Magdalene welcomed the quietness of the gardens. But time still moved too slowly for her, underscoring the heavy sense of doom in her spirit.

She turned to Joanna as they walked. "Will Chuza know when they have arrested Jesus?"

"Perhaps. And perhaps not. But if he does—"

"I wonder if the others are with him?" Magdalene cut in, seeming not to hear Joanna's answer to her first question. "Peter, John, James, and the others?"

"It would be a surprise if they were not."

"Do you think they will arrest him at the place where he celebrates his Passover supper tonight?"

"I don't know," Joanna said.

"I think I want to know."

Joanna stopped walking and put a restraining hand on her arm. "Magdalene. Stop torturing yourself."

The words struck at her heart. "I love him, Joanna. I don't want to lose him." She hid her face in her hands and sobbed, shaking with a sadness deeper than any she had ever known. Joanna embraced her friend and held her tightly until the tears of fear and sorrow slowed and finally stanched themselves.

The afternoon waned. A strong wind rose from the north and urged them to retire to the palace. They did so, accompanied by the spectre of grief to come.

During the night Magdalene slept fitfully. Thoughts of Jesus and Domenicus, of Fortunatas and Chuza, of Joanna and herself and Jesus, of her parents and Jesus, of Susanna and James, and of herself and Jesus were at the threshold of her wakefulness. They were incomplete thoughts, more like snatches of memories, vague and drifting and overlaid with a mist of danger and suffering.

They were still with her when she awoke to the brilliant sun of yet another day, the beginning of the Jews' Passover.

Her thoughts now focused on Jesus. Was he still free? Was he at the Temple worshipping? Or was he on the Temple Mount teaching and preaching and healing? Or had the dreaded arrest occurred? Was he imprisoned somewhere in the Holy City? Surely, Chuza would know this. And if he knew, Joanna would know.

She got out of bed, washed her face at one of the bowls the servants had placed in her sleeping compartment, dressed, and went into another room of the apartment in search of Joanna.

She found her in a small sitting room with Chuza, Tobias and Fortunatas. They were in intense conversation. Instantly, she knew they had to be talking about Jesus. Something dreadful already had happened. She knew it in her spirit. She stood quite still just inside the doorway, yearning to know what had happened—needing to know—yet dreading to ask.

Fortunatas straightened and stood up as if to leave, then noticed her standing at the doorway. He said something, and the others turned to look at her. Joanna's cheeks glistened with tears. With a frown, Fortunatas walked toward her.

Magdalene felt her heart pound with dread. "They have arrested Jesus, haven't they?"

He nodded.

"When?"

"Last night."

"Where?"

"In the garden on the Mount of Olives."

"Where have they imprisoned him? And can I visit him?"

Behind Fortunatas, Joanna stood up and came toward her.

"Where have they imprisoned him?" Magdalene asked again.

Fortunatas looked at the floor, unable to answer.

"He is not in prison, Magdalene," Joanna said, her eyes blurred with moisture.

"But Fortunatas said he had been arrested . . . "

Chuza came to her, great sadness in his face. "They have already held his trial. In the early hours before dawn. And he has been condemned for high treason and heresy."

Fortunatas found his voice. "At this moment, he is carrying his cross to the Place of Skulls."

It was as if time stopped. The room was hushed in shocked disbelief, yet Magdalene felt waves of horror and denial flooding her senses, much as she had experienced so often before at the onset of one of her terrifying spells. She put out a hand to steady herself in the doorway and drew several deep breaths to fight off the pounding inside her chest.

"Crucified?" she heard herself ask in a faraway voice, and then her mind screamed denial. No! It could not be so! No! No! No!

Instinctively she braced herself for the dreaded spell that always came in moments such as this one . . . but when her mind stayed clear of the blackness she realized, *He has indeed healed me and made me whole. But now this—is this the way we repay him for all the good he has brought to us?*

Joanna came to embrace her. Magdalene backed away, looked at each one of them with unseeing eyes, and heard herself say, "I must go to him. I must be with him. He must know that I care about him."

"You cannot go to that awful place," Chuza said.

"I must be with him. He must know that I love him enough to come to him."

Chuza once again started to protest. But Joanna placed a gentle hand on his arm, and slowly shook her head. She turned then to Magdalene. "I will go with you."

"As will I," said Fortunatas.

"We will all go with you," Chuza reluctantly agreed, motioning for Razis and Eglah to bring wraps for the women.

It was well past the sixth hour by the time they arrived at the place of doom outside the city walls north and west of the palace. A crowd of people was already there, standing back a respectful distance from a cordon of spear-wielding Roman soldiers. Magdalene knew some of them, remembering their faces from the crowds that had followed Jesus around Galilee.

She saw John, with an arm around Jesus' mother—a small woman whose beautiful face now reflected agony. John's own mother, Salome, was there too. But where were the others, Magdalene wondered. Where was James, and Peter, Thomas and Matthew, and the rest of the twelve? Why were they not here?

The Place of Skulls was a small hillock, isolated and bare of all vegetation, as if nature herself was aware that this was a place to be avoided and that no living thing should grow on it or soften its barrenness.

On its crest, three crosses of rough-hewn timber had been erected. On each of these was nailed a living human being. Two thieves right and left. And in the center, Jesus. His outstretched arms were nailed to the cross-timber at the wrists. His feet were nailed to the rough wooden upright. Above his head, a crudely printed sign insolently proclaimed: *Jesus of Nazareth, King of the Jews.* A crown of thorns had been thrust scornfully onto his head, pressed so deeply into the flesh that the blood poured down his face and over his chest.

Magdalene stopped abruptly at the sight of him, her heart crying out in anguish. She wished she hadn't come. She wanted to turn and run, to erase from her eyes the sight of him hanging there. She cried out in disbelieving horror at what she saw, hoping that this might only be some awful dream from which she would awake, but knowing that it was all too real. Her dear friend, Jesus of

Nazareth, the man who healed the sick and preached love and forgiveness, was suffering the most horrible execution ever devised by mankind.

Laughter, harsh and obscene, abruptly erupted from the foot of the cross. There, Roman soldiers gambled for Jesus' clothing while they made jokes about him.

Magdalene fought against the horror, shuddered and forced herself to open her eyes. Jesus was struggling to breathe. He stirred, and spoke to his mother and to John.

"Mother, here is thy son. Son, here is thy mother."

Several among the crowd, understanding the legacy of Jesus' words, recognizing the generosity of his concern for his mother, began to mutter aloud at the senselessness of his coming death. Some of the soldiers, already nervous, now made threatening gestures toward the crowd with their spears and lances. The crowd quieted and stepped back from the cordon of soldiers.

Again Jesus stirred, raising himself with his pierced feet to gasp for breath. He turned his head in Magdalene's direction.

Her heart caught in her throat. Did she imagine it or did an emanation of supernatural energy still pulse from him? Did she imagine it or had he smiled at her?

Clouds formed without warning. The skies darkened. Sunlight dimmed and the chill in the wind increased.

Magdalene pulled her cloak closer and welcomed the protective arm which Fortunatas placed around her shoulders.

Jesus lifted himself again. From his lips now came the cry, *"Eli, Eli, Lama Sabachthani?"*

"Father, Father, Why have you forsaken me?" Magdalene repeated, her voice wrenching with despair. Fortunatas pulled her closer and held her more firmly, as if the gesture should reassure and comfort.

Members of the crowd began to moan and murmur. A group of women on the far side of the cross started a mournful wailing. Deeper came the blackness of the sky. Distant thunder foreshadowed a dying spirit.

Once more Jesus stirred. His lips moved, but his words were barely audible: "It is finished."

Far away across the rooftops of the holy city of Jerusalem came the familiar, haunting sound of ram's horn trumpets as the priests on the Temple Mount proclaimed the ninth hour of the day. One of the Roman soldiers at the foot of the cross stood up, stretched and walked away down the hill. His companion watched him go, cursed, got to his feet and turned to look up at Jesus.

"Is he dead yet?" asked a third soldier, poking at Jesus with his spear.

"If not, soon will be," said the second soldier as he drove his lance hard into Jesus' side. The crowd gasped as blood and water gushed from the wound.

Magdalene sagged against Fortunatas, drained of strength, emptied of hope. Jesus was dead. That beautiful, loving man, her friend and healer, was dead. What kind of a world was it that killed a man such as this?

Joanna hid her face against Chuza's shoulder.

The third soldier spat as he watched his companion jerk the lance free from Jesus' body. "Didn't even have to break his legs. Now the Jews can come and take him down."

"Good thing," replied the other. "Or else they wouldn't bury him until after their Sabbath."

Now the clouds fully covered the face of the sky, cloaking the Place of Skulls in darkness. Thunder and lightning raged from the heavens as if the voice of God Himself was condemning the evil of mankind.

Then the rains came, hard and scouring, matching the tears of horror and sadness that had flowed from most of those who had kept the vigil of death. And most began to turn away. John insisted that his mother and the mother of Jesus follow him to a place of shelter. The Roman officer in charge of the cordon of soldiers dismissed them. They ran to find refuge from the pelting rain. Soon, the only people remaining at the foot of the cross were Magdalene, Joanna, Chuza, Tobias and Fortunatas.

As they turned to leave, they saw two men with their servants climbing the hill. The newcomers arrived at the center cross and braced a ladder against the cross-timber. Gently, they removed Jesus' body and lowered him to the mud below.

"We know those men," Chuza said, a tone of surprise in his voice. "That's Joseph, of Arimathea—and Nicodemus the banker." He called out to them, "Joseph, where are you taking Jesus?"

"To my sepulchre beyond the hill there," Joseph replied. "It is a new tomb. I had it prepared for my own body. But my friend, the young rabbi, precedes me to the heavenly place." He hesitated, turned and looked at Magdalene and Joanna. "Will your wife and her friend see to him until the Sabbath is passed?"

Chuza nodded. "Yes, they will want to. My wife's

friend, the Lady Magdalene, is a woman whom Jesus healed. They will attend him."

"Good. Nicodemus has brought the necessary mixture of myrrh and aloes and the strips of linens they will need." The merchant paused and looked quizzically at Chuza. "You truly are a Jesus-believer, aren't you?"

A resigned smile broke over Chuza's round face. "How could I be otherwise, since I do not believe in cruelty to men who heal and preach peace." He turned and motioned for Joanna, Magdalene, Tobias and Fortunatas to follow them as Jesus' body was carried to the Arimathean's nearby tomb.

The servants laid Jesus' body carefully on the stone platform inside the tomb and handed dry rags and linens to Magdalene and the bag of spices to Joanna. Then they backed away so the women could put in place the spices and the linen strips.

Magdalene fought back a fresh wave of tears as she knelt beside Jesus and pulled the hateful crown of thorns from his head. She laid it aside, then gently dabbed at the puncture wounds it had made and wiped the rain and blood from his face. Heartbroken as she was, she found solace in helping care for him. She realized that even now—after rejection, humiliation, physical abuse and death—there was strength in the line of his brow, generosity in the open planes of his face, and grace in the line of his mouth from which had poured the wisdom of the One True God.

Lovingly, she took his hands in her own, remembering how strong and good they were—working hands, hands of inordinate power, hands of tenderness and healing. Her tears stung her eyes and spattered down where his hands were entwined with hers.

Joanna touched her shoulder. "We must go now, Magdalene. Jesus would not want us to violate the Jewish Sabbath. We will come back to finish our work with the spices and linens."

Reluctantly, Magdalene rose to her feet and followed Joanna out of the tomb. The Arimathean's servants rolled the great stone into place at the tomb's entrance, closing it off. A few feet away, several Roman soldiers had gathered to stand guard.

Chuza bade farewell to Joseph the Arimathean and Nicodemus the banker, and led the women, Fortunatas, and Tobias back into the city.

The next days were hazy with numbness, denial, heartache. Neither Magdalene nor her friends were able to lift the pall of grief that hovered over the household and gripped their hearts. Time passed slowly. People tried to go about their daily tasks, but their movements and conversations were dream-like.

Early on the third day, while it was still dark, Magdalene rose and left the apartment. She had told Joanna the night before that she wished to have a few moments alone in the garden before they entered the tomb to complete the work on Jesus' body. She wished to sit in the garden and think of him and mourn him alone. With her usual compassion, Joanna had understood and agreed. And so it was that Magdalene slipped away from the palace by a side door, made her way through the pre-dawn gloom to the Place of Tombs and, in particular, to the tomb where Jesus' body lay.

As she neared the location, she became momentarily confused and stopped. There was no great stone at the entrance to the tomb she thought Jesus was in. And no soldiers. Fear caught at her. Who could have moved the stone? And why? In a panic, she turned and fled.

Coming down the hill toward her were Peter and John. She ran to them, crying out, "They have taken our Lord out of the tomb. Where could they have put him?"

Peter brushed her aside and began to run toward the tomb. John joined the chase, caught up with Peter and passed him. He didn't stop running until he had entered the tomb and searched its corners. "She's right, Peter. He is gone. Nothing is here but strips of linen and some spices!"

Now Peter went into the tomb. Within seconds he exited, pale with disbelief. He pulled on John's arm and the two ran back up the hill toward the house where they were staying.

Magdalene watched them go, then slowly walked back down the hill toward the tomb. The closer she came to it, the more unnerved she felt. In the past few days she had cried so much that she wondered if there were any more tears inside her, but now the hurt choked at her and her tears blurred with a fresh outpouring of grief and despair. She pulled a square of linen from her sash and wiped at her eyes. Still, the tears came. Was crucifixion not enough of a disgrace? Did they have to further dishonor him by stealing away his body?

She bent to look into the tomb herself, and shook her head in disbelief. No. It couldn't be. She dabbed at her eyes to clear her vision and looked again. What was it? *Who* was it? Seated on the stone bench where Jesus' body had been were two men dressed in purest white. She stared in astonishment.

"Woman, why are you crying?" asked one of the men. He seemed to be *smiling.*

The question seemed presumptuous, but Magdalene answered plainly, "They have taken away my Lord. I don't know where they have put him."

Before either of the men in the tomb could speak further, she saw a movement in the corner of her eye. She turned to see the gardener standing before her.

"If you have carried him away, tell me where you have put him and I will get him," she pleaded.

As the man spoke, he turned so she could see his face. "Magdalene, do you not know me?"

Her heart leapt. "Jesus?"

He smiled.

"Rabboni!" She went toward him, her hands outstretched in loving welcome.

He backed away. "Do not touch me. Do not hold on to me. For I have not yet returned to the Father. Go instead to my brothers and tell them, 'I am returning to my Father, and to your Father, to my God and to your God.'"

Still stunned, she nodded her obedience, then looked again to see his eyes. He had disappeared. Had she dreamed it? No, this was no dream. He was alive! She suddenly recalled what he had said to her and to many others who followed him: "I am the resurrection and the life." He was real. He was alive. She had seen him! He had spoken to her, and she to him. *He lives!* she cried to herself. *Jesus lives!*

She turned and hurried up the hill to find his men and give them the news, the wonderful news that Jesus was alive. But after she had told her story, they looked at her as if she was mad. Obviously they did not believe her.

She shrugged off their disbelief, then challenged them. "I have given you Jesus' message, as he asked me to do. If you don't believe it is real, it is not me you doubt, but Jesus, your Lord!"

She turned, left the house where they were staying and ran toward the palace to share the news with Joanna and the others. As she ran, her mind skipped backward to her girlhood, to a time when all she had ever wanted from life was to be free of her dreaded spells and to know there was someone who would love her forever, and whom she could love forever. Now Jesus had made both dreams a reality. She had not lost him. Not even to death. What was more wonderful, she realized that she never would.

A NOTE TO THE READER

This book was selected by the book division of the company that publishes *Guideposts*, a monthly magazine filled with true stories of people's adventures in faith.

If you have found inspiration in this book, we think you'll find monthly help and inspiration in the exciting stories that appear in our magazine.

Guideposts is not sold on the newsstand. It's available by subscription only. And subscribing is easy. All you have to do is write Guideposts, 39 Seminary Hill Road, Carmel, New York 10512. For those with special reading needs, *Guideposts* is published in Big Print, Braille, and Talking Magazine.

When you subscribe, each month you can count on receiving exciting new evidence of God's presence and His abiding love for His people.

Guideposts is also available on the Internet by accessing our homepage on the World Wide Web at http://www.guideposts.org. Send prayer requests to our Monday morning Prayer Fellowship. Read stories from recent issues of our magazines, *Guideposts*, *Angels on Earth, Guideposts for Kids* and *Positive Living*, and follow our popular book of daily devotionals, *Daily Guideposts*. Excerpts from some of our best-selling books are also available.